WHO LET THE ANIMAL OUT?

Author: Andre Calvin Lee Jr.

Who Let The Animal Out?

Dedication
To my pops Draco Dee, my Uncle Doc, and Grandma
Daisy may your spirits resonate in my journey. My moms,
siblings, my 8 Mile family and my spiritual family,
dreams are only visions we haven't touched yet.

FRESH OUT

I walked out of the Greyhound Station in downtown Detroit feeling like a new man. I was 16 years old when I shot a dude in the chest; he robbed my little cousin Mark for his shoes. I was sentenced to five years for attempted murder, I did my first two years in Maxey Boys Training School in Whitmore Lake, Michigan. Which in my opinion wasn't nothing but a baby prison, preparing you for real prison. Once I was 18, I was transferred to Thumbs Prison in Lapeer, Michigan. Thumbs' prison housed the worst juvenile offenders in Michigan. It was so wild in Thumbs, so wild, that the guards knick-named it Gladiator School. I'd rather die before I go back to prison.

So, with that in mind, I shook them thoughts out of my mind and looked around for my ride. I heard a horn honking an I spotted an all-white caddy truck pulling up. My Auntie Pam stepped out, looking just like the dope mans' wife.

"Oh my God, Ali you big as shit boy. I barely recognized yo ass. Give me a hug boy." I smiled, gave my Auntie a hug, then jumped in the caddy, plus it was cold as shit. We pulled off. "Damn Ali, your uncle and cousin gone be so happy to see you. Oh, and I see you received the clothes I sent you."

"Yeah, Auntie Pam I appreciate it too. I would have never made it out there if it wasn't for you."

"You don't have to thank me boy, matter-of-fact fuck that, thank me by not taking yo crazy ass back okay, can you do that?"

I laughed and nodded my head. I looked in the back and noticed a bunch of bags from different stores. "Damn Auntie it look like you just left the mall. What, you didn't like yo wardrobe?" I asked.

"Boy Bye! My wardrobe the shit, I picked that up for you." My eyes got big as shit, she just laughed.

"What, I know you ain't think I was going to have my nephew walking around with one outfit, did you?" With that being said, she threw on her shades, even though it was January and no sun out; turned up the radio and drove faster. I was shocked but, not surprised, my Auntie looked out for me the whole time locked up but, I'm home now and I'm a grown ass man. Fuck a handout, I'm a get my own. Shit… next time I'm taking her ass shopping.

FAMILY

Chapter 2

We pulled up to a nice-looking house round 7 Mile, between Southfield and Evergreen, on Warwick St. First thing I noticed was another white caddy truck, but longer than my aunties and an Audi truck in the driveway. "Who live here, Auntie?"

"This your cousin Mark house. That's his Audi truck in the driveway and that's Big Rome's long sleeve right there."

I didn't know what a long sleeve was, but I didn't want to seem slow, so I just nodded and jumped out. Me and Auntie both grabbed as many bags as we could and walked toward the house. Before we got to the door Mark came out looking mad. Once he noticed us, he smiled and took the bags from Auntie Pam and went in the house.

Mark Shouted, "aye pops, momma back with Ali and he big as shit."

"Watch yo mouth boy, you ain't grown."

Mark laughed and came and gave me a hug.

"Man cuz, it's good to see you, man I missed you."

"Yea, I missed you too, Mark. Good lookin out, on them pictures you sent me cuz." Before he could respond, I heard a toilet flush and Uncle Rome came out the bathroom washing his hands.

Now, Big Rome's one of the biggest heroin dealers on the west side. He also, happens to be married to my Auntie and Marks father. Big Rome look like LL Cool J in the movie, *In Too Deep*. Big, bald-headed, with muscles and a lot of money. My Auntie Pam favors Lisa Raye, so she walks around with her nose in the air, but hey she family. I looked at Mark, he's about 5'10, 175 pounds, with a receding hairline. He kind of looked like the real Alpo from the *Paid in Full* story. I smiled to myself.

"Lil Ali, what's poppin Nephew? Glad you could finally join us in the free world." He smiled one of those smiles, that makes you feel relaxed around him.

"Yea Unk, it feels good to be home. Trust me, I'm not never going back. Now that I'm home, I'm just trying to earn my fair share."

Big Rome nodded like he understood what I was saying. "Yeah Nephew I understand, a part of being a man means being able to earn his own. Me and your cousin was just having a similar conversation before you got here, but you have to remember not to move too fast. You have heard of the sayin 'why run down to fuck one cow, when we can walk down and fuck'em all?'"

I shook my head and looked at Mark who looked irritated, like he heard this a million times. I glanced at Auntie Pam, and she wasn't even paying attention to us. She was lost in her phone like most females.

"Look nephew" Big Rome said, "its rules to this game we in that most young guys don't abide by. If you learn and listen you can make it far in this game, just remember to take it slow. Remember the P's nephew."

"What's the P's Unk?"

"Proper, planning, prevents, poor, performance." I nodded my head because it made sense.

"Well, we're about to get up out of here. I know ya'll got a lot of things to catch up on." Big Rome said, as him and Auntie Pam gave us hugs and left.

"Man cuz, sorry about that man. You know my Pop's love preaching and shit he be gettin on my nerves with that shit." Mark said, while he passed me the blunt.

We were driving on our way to the hood on Fenkell and Livernois, where we grew up at.

"I ain't trippin cuz. Unk was just droppin some jewels on us, he ain't said shit wrong." Mark didn't respond, he just continued to drive while I was in deep thought.

"Look cuz you been gone for a long-time fool and a lot of shit changed, but don't trip I got yo back."

"Shit cuz, it ain't changed that much. Money still the motivation ain't it?" I had to ask cuz, I was confused at what he was gettin at.

"Yea you right, but the shit people out here doin to get it has changed. It ain't all about Dope Niggas robbin, cashing fake checks, identity theft everything. In this game we in though, the old rules still apply. Stack, pray, and stay out the way."

I just sat there and listened to Mark tell me what was what in the streets, but I only half listened. I was stuck on how Mark and Big Rome both used the words "In this game we in," like I was a dope boy or something. I ain't never sold drugs in my life and I didn't plan to start now. Imma animal by nature and I need to eat. When we say "eat" in my city we mean rob, steal, and kill. For now, imma let the animal rest. Just for now though, one thing about an animal sooner or later their instincts always win.

WHITE PARTY

Chapter 3

We rode around the hood for a minute. Mostly Mark was just droppin off dope and picking up money. Somebody mentioned something about a white party and Mark got all geeked up about it, so we drove to his house to start getting dressed.

"I'm tellin you cuz, a white party at Silver Rain, trust me we fin-da have fun nigga; enjoy ourselves for yo first day home," Mark boasted.

"What the fuck is Silver Rain Mark?"

"A titty bar cuz, that bitch be off the hook. I fuck with a lil bitch in there, so we good. Plus, it's yo first day home I gotta get yo ass some pussy cuz." I guess he thought that was funny because he started laughing hard as shit. He looked at me and noticed I wasn't laughing and said, "Naw I'm bullshitin cuz. Go jump in the shower and imma throw you some gear on your bed."

"Auntie got me some shit cuz."

"Naw, I got some all-white shit for you. It's brand new so don't trip, we fin-da clown in that bitch tonight." I took about a 15-minute shower walked in the bedroom and sure enough, Mark had a whole outfit for me laid out. I heard a knock on the door. "Aye cuz, here go a box of condoms. You don't wanna end up like me with a crazy ass B.M." With that he closed the door and left. I tossed the condoms on the dresser and started getting dressed.

I turned and looked at myself in a full-length mirror and smiled. I was about 5'11, 200 pounds, no fat, all muscle from working out for five years. I have light brown skin, green eyes that I guess I got from my father, and I let my beard grow out, so most people assumed, I was a Sunni Muslim. I wasn't though, I didn't believe in any religion. Some people might say I'm an atheist, but I'm just me; plain and simple. I put on my clothes, walked out the room and found Mark already dressed sitting on the couch waiting on me.

"Damn Nigga, I thought I was gone have to come and drag yo ass out of there fool." He laughed and passed me the blunt.

I hit it real hard and instantly, started choking. Damn! This some good weed, I guess cuz had the best of everything.

"Slow down fool, that ain't that Reggie Bush you was smoking back in the day." This time we both laughed because he was right. "Oh yea, cuz here hold this." He reached under the couch and passed me a baby 40 cal, all black and wasn't even bigger than my hand.

"Damn cuz good lookin out. What, I'm posed to take it wit us?" I asked.

"Hell yea fool, lets ride" He got up to leave, but I didn't budge.

"Mark! Where the fuck do I put this gun with these tight ass clothes you got me wearing?" Again, he laughed at me.

"Naw cuz, that's the swag now. You funny, just put it in your back pocket and let's slide."

I did as I was told, we both jump in the Audi truck and sped off. When we pulled into the parking lot of Silver Rain, Mark turned the car off and turned toward me....

"Look cuz, here go five bands for you to go crazy with tonight. Now you with me so naturally the hoes gone be on you, but so will the Jack Boyz. We fin-da go in this bitch and make a mess, but keep yo eyes open, you got that?"

"Fasho cuz, you know I'm on point."

"Alright bet! Now, let's go make these niggas mad."

When we jumped out the car I noticed the long line and bouncers checking people, so I grabbed mark. "Aye cuz, how Imma sneak this banger in?"

"Don't even trip cuz, rich niggas don't wait in line or get searched. Just follow my lead." We walked past the line and instantly niggas started mugging us. Mark walked up to the bouncer shook his hand with a couple 100-dollar bills in it and like that, we was in. When we got in it was like a whole nother world. All the women were either naked or close to it. All the niggas were dressed in white, throwing money on every stripper that walked by. A red bone stripper looked at me and winked.

Mark was gettin hugs and kisses from every

ANDRE CALVIN LEE JR

chick he walked by, like he was a rapper and I figured out why? Mark was dressed in an all-white *Balmain* outfit with some 2,500-dollar all-white, Red *Bottom Christian Louboutin's*. He had a big ass icy chain that had the numbers 4 and 1 on it for our hood Fenkell of 5 Mile. On top of that he wore a pair of all-white *Cartier* glasses that everyone in Detroit called Buffs with lots of diamonds in the nose piece and a presidential *Rolex* to put the icing on the cake. I'm not no hater, I liked seeing Mark floss. Plus, he hooked me up also. I was wearing some all-white *True Religion* pants, all white *Gucci* shoes, and an all-white *Gucci* sweater. I topped it off with some *Gucci* glasses and bitches thought I was a rapper, too. We grabbed a booth in the V.I.P and a sexy ass waitress came to take our order.

"Hey Mark, I shoulda knew yo as was gone be here tonight. What you drinkin?"

"Hell yea, you know I came to show up and show out. Grab me a fifth of Patron, and.... cuz what you sippin, Remy?"

"Yea, Remy cool."

"Okay, and grab cuz a fifth of 1738." Mark said, as he handed the waitress a stack of hundreds.

"Damn Mark, you rude as shit, you not gone introduce me to yo friend." The waitress made a face like she was fake mad.

"Oh, my fault lil mama. Lala, this my big cousin Ali; he just got out the joint today, cuz this is Lala."

I nodded at her coolly she smiled and asked,

"how long was you locked up?

"Too long baby girl, way too long."

"Oh yea, well I get off a 2:00. If you a big tipper maybe me and my home girl will give you a private coming home party," Lala asked me seductively.

"I'll keep that in mind sexy."

"I bet you will." I had to smile shortly, had too much confidence. Before she walked away Mark stopped her again.

"Aye lil mama, where Peaches at?"

"Oh she in the back, I'll tell her you out here."

"Cool and while you at it bring me and cuz back 1,000 in ones a piece," Mark said then gave her 10 hundred-dollar bills. She looked at me, so I followed suit and passed her 1,000 dollars, also. I could almost see the dollar signs in her eyes. Lala walked to the back and Mark fired up two blunts and past one to me. I smoked as I also looked over the crowd. I felt eyes on us and just like Mark said, the strippers wasn't the only people keeping a close eye on us.

After a short while I noticed Lala coming back toward us with both our drinks on a platter, but what caught my eye was the gorgeous red bone following her. She was tall, at least 5'10. She looked like Alicia Keys with the ass to match. She walked with an air of confidence that demanded attention. A couple of guys tried to stop her, but she never even looked their way. Lala walked up and sat our drinks down and light skin, just sat there and waited. "Here you go Mark, here Ali. Oh, and here go ya'll money."

14

Lala said as she reached in the bag she was carrying and started putting stacks of one-dollar bills on the table.

"Good lookin out Lala. When you done working grab up Diamond and we gone slide to my crib tonight," Mark said to Lala, but never took his eyes off of light skin.

"Okay Mark, see you later Ali."

"Fasho" I said once Lala walked off.

Light skin sat down next to mark and kissed him hard as shit. "Damn baby slow down I can't breathe," Mark said smiling. "Bae, this my cousin Ali I was tellin you about, cuz this is my Wife Peaches."

"Oh my God, I'm so embarrassed I heard a lot about you," Peaches said to me.

"I heard a lot about you too, nice to meet you also." She smiled like I knew she would. Truthfully, Mark never mentioned peaches to me, but I could tell she obviously meant a lot to him, so I stroked her ego. Mark peeped me and nodded toward me nonchalantly.

We sat for a couple of hours throwing money and talking shit. Around 1:50 am people started clearing out, so we gathered our belongings and prepared to leave. I noticed Lala approaching with a dark skinned sexy sista and I assumed she was Diamond.

"Diamond, Lala, you ready to slide," Mark asked.

So I was right, they both nodded and headed to the door. I don't know how to explain it; I don't even know what to call it, but I got a feeling in the middle of my gut that trouble was near. I slid my hand in my back pocket and cuffed the gun. I scanned the crowd and noticed a black ass Shawty Lo looking nigga, mugging the shit out of Mark, and approaching us real fast. He had one of his hands slightly behind his leg, so I couldn't see what was in it. He reached a handout to grab Mark, who wasn't paying attention at all and before I knew it the animal came out of me. I grabbed his hand and slapped him hard as shit with the pistol. He hit the ground and a champagne bottle shattered all over the floor! Pussy people started screaming and running past me out the door, while I pistol whipped Shawty Lo ass unconscious. I put the gun under his chin about to blow his shit off, when I felt some strong hands grab me from behind.

"Cuz, you made yo point now calm down before you make a mistake in here," Mark argued.

"Naw Mark, ain't no mistakes I'm fin-da show this pussy nigga what happen when he fuck with fam," I was pissed.

"Ali! It's to many fuckin witnesses in here cuz. I don't want to see you go back to jail cuz, damn." Once he said my name I started to calm down, not because he was right. I stopped just because he said my name. I put the pistol up and walked out the club. Mark gave a guy who I assume owned the club a bunch of money. We made it to the truck safe jumped in and left.

While mark was driving, Peaches was in the

passenger side complaining about losing her job. I was in the back between Lala and Diamond and both of them were drunk as shit.

"Ooooh yo name Ali, like the fighter huh," Diamond asked me.

"Naw I'm Ali. Just Ali, nobody else," I said in a calm voice. She made a face and turned and looked out the window.

Shortly after we arrived at Marks house and we all stumbled in drunk as shit. Mark told Peaches to go in his room and Diamond and Lala went to mines and waited.

"Aye cuz, I appreciate you havin my back man for real," Mark said with his eyes were low as shit.

"Don't mention it cuz, I know you woulda did the same for me," I responded.

"Yea cuz I woulda, but fuck that shit I love you Ali. Welcome home. Now, go in there and fuck the shit out them bitches. They both paid for." With that Mark smiled and walked into his room and shut the door.

Now, I ain't no virgin neither am I scared of pussy, but I was nervous as shit. I ain't never fucked two bitches before let alone, two bad bitches. I took a deep breath turned my swag on and walked into my room. Damn, I don't know what I expected, but it wasn't this. Both Diamond and Lala asshole naked in the 69-position eating each other out. Lala looked at me and asked, "what, you just gone stand there?" Say no more. I got naked quick as shit and laid across the bed. Dick standing straight up, both women took turns seeing who could swallow my 10 inches; both of them lost. Then Diamond started sucking my dick hard and slow while Lala got up and sat right on my face. Now I ain't no dummy, I know these hoes probably fuck a different nigga every night, but I was high, drunk, caught up in the moment, and fresh home. Fuck it. You only live once right? Diamond sucking my dick, I grabbed Lala by bother ass cheeks and ate that pussy like shrimp fried rice. I came hard as shit in Diamond mouth, and she didn't waste a drop. Lala jumped off my face and left my beard soaked full of cum. My head was spinning like crazy, and I was tired as shit, but Diamond started sucking right back on my dick till I got back hard. She tried to get on top to ride me, but I stopped her.

"Hold on lil mama, what the fuck you doin?"

She looked at me crazy and said, "nigga you ain't been locked up that long I'm fin-da fuck the shit out you," Diamond boasted.

I flipped her off of me quick as shit. She looked stunned. I grabbed her by her legs and flipped her on her stomach. Once I grabbed her by her waist, she got the picture, bent over on her knees, and arched her back sexy as shit. I smacked her on the ass hard as hell and stuck my dick in, her pussy was wet as fuck. I started hittin the pussy hard as shit, she was screaming loud. I pushed her head down into Lalas' pussy and she started eating her good-good again. I looked up and saw the box of condoms Mark gave me earlier on the dresser, Oops!! Oh Well, better luck next time. I made them bitches switch positions

then I started beating up Lalas' Pussy. Yea, welcome
home fasho.

UNDERSTANDING THE RULES

Chapter 4

I woke up the nest morning to voices in the Livingroom. Whoever it was, they were arguing with Mark, but their voices were muffled. Without even thinking instinct made me slide out of bed to get the gun out of my pants pocket. I looked over at Lala and Diamond and they were sleeping like angels. I put my ear to the door trying to see if I could hear something. I couldn't, so I cracked the door as quietly as I could. When I looked out the door, I saw Mark in a heated conversation with some chick who had a little boy in her hands. The little boy looked like Mark spit him out. Baby Mama! She was short like maybe 5'5, nice thick body, brown skin, with dreadlocks that came down her ass. Drop dead gorgeous!

"Damn nigga that bitch pussy that good you pistol whippin niggas in the club."

"Keisha, slow yo hot ass down, get yo facts straight, I ain't do shit, and last I checked bitch you had a nigga, so why you so mad?"

Keisha just starred at Mark for about 20

seconds with a dumb look on her face then she spazzed out.

"Nigga, I ain't got time for no nigga. I got a son with a dead-beat ass nigga, who think he the shit," Kesha fused.

"First off bitch I ain't no dead bead; my son don't want for shit. "Mark was gettin heated up, too.

"Yea you spend money but learn to spend time, dummy."

"I'm not gone keep tellin you to watch yo mouth Keisha, go talk that shit to yo man."

"Who Mark? Who am I fucking now?"

"Okay you want to go there, you don't think I know you been duckin the nigga Juice, huh" Mark asked hesitantly. He must a nerve because Keisha had the dumb look on her face, again. "Yea bitch, now you lookin stupid," Mark said.

"Fuck you Mark! I'm leaving Lil Mark here I got a job interview, so spend some time with yo son lame!"

Keisha spazzed out on Mark, then put Lil Mark down and walked out the door. Mark tried to stop her from leaving, but it was too late. She was gone. I felt like a female for ease dropping like that.

So, I put on some shorts and walked out to the Livingroom. "Damn what's up cuz, you look tired as shit. Damn boy, that lil nigga look just like you," I said looking at Lil Mark.

"Yea man, this my lil man; he only 3 years old. Mark this yo big cousin Ali, show him how old you are," Mark said.

Lil Mark tried to put up three fingers like kids do. He used his right hand to hold down two fingers on his left then said "three." Me and mark laughed and that made Lil Mark laugh. I instantly fell in love with my baby cousin.

Peaches came out the bathroom with nothing on, but some flip flops. Mark didn't seem to mind and neither did she. She poured some Kool-Aid and walked back in Mark room. Damn.

"Yea cuz that shit that happened last night at the bar all in the streets," Mark told me.

"I don't give a fuck cuz. If a nigga want some smoke I'm the right nigga to play with. Who was that nigga anyway?" Before Mark could answer me we heard a loud knock on the door. I side stepped out the way in case someone started shootin threw the door, then I pulled my strap out and pointed it toward the door.

Mark had a confused look on his face. "Ali, what the fuck is you doing?" Mark got up and opened the door and I saw Big Rome and Auntie Pam at the door. I felt stupid as fuck.

"Don't nobody know where I stay bro, we good," Mark told me.

Auntie Pam came in said hi to me and Mark. She scooped up baby Mark and started kissing him all over his face. "Oh my God Rome, look at my grandson so pretty," Auntie Pam said still kissing him.

"Bae, why don't you take baby Mark to get some ice cream while I holla at the boys real quick,"

Big Rome said to Auntie Pam. With that she scooped up baby Mark and walked out the door.

Once Auntie Pam was gone we all just sat there in silence. Big Rome looked like he was in deep thought. Mark was rolling a blunt, his whole demeanor told me that he was pissed. Big Rome took a deep breath then looked at Mark and said, "Tell me what happened and don't lie." Mark explained the story step by step play by play. Once he was done Big Rome looked at me then back to Mark.

"Did you tell yo cousin why you and Twerk got a problem," Big Rome asked Mark. Mark just put his head down and shook his head. Big Rome looked at me. "Nephew, what yo cousin forgot to tell you is that peaches use to be Twerks girl, Mark took her, and it's been bad blood ever since. He also forgot to tell you Twerk ain't no small-time hustler. We do business together and I know for a fact, that he has people that love to kill for him!"

"To be honest Unk, and I don't mean no disrespect to you, but Mark my family. I thought he had a gun I shoulda killed his ass. What type of man try to sneak you with a champagne bottle?" Mark giggled a lil bit, but when Big Rome looked at him he shut up.

Big Rome fumed "I'm not debating rather or not you did the wrong or right thing, Ali. I'm sayin the way you did it was hot and stupid." Now I was getting pissed off.

"Unk, fuck that nigga. Show me where that nigga be, and I'll kill his ass and whoever ridin wit him." Big Rome smiled at what I said and that I almost checked his ass. Calm down, Ali. Take a deep breath.

"Let me tell you something nephew. I don't know if you believe in God or not, but I'm fin-da breath on you right quick," Big Rome said. I didn't say shit, so he continued, "the greatest trick the devil ever did was making people believe he didn't exist."

Now I was really lost. What the fuck did the devil got to do with me? Big Rome must have seen the confused look on my face, so he explained further.

"Let me explain it for you, nephew. The game that we in requires for us to stay under the radar. The move that you pulled on Twerk last night made everybody around think that you the shooter for Mark," Big Mark said.

I shrugged my shoulder because I figured that I was the shooter for Mark. He was my only family besides Auntie Pam. Big Rome my uncle through marriage, but that ain't the same as blood.

"I see the devil in yo eyes nephew. I see a killer ready to be unleashed, but if you want to stay alive and thrive. You need to think smarter; make people think you soft or lame," Big Rome said to me. "But, when it's time to do dirt you do it by yo self, make sure yo face is never seen, and leave no witnesses. Once people think that you the shooter Ali, if it's a problem then you gone be the first person that the enemy feels he has to kill first; because you're the biggest threat."

Now I understand what he meant. Big Rome was smart as shit and once I put my pride to the side and listened I realized that everything he was tellin me was the rules to stayin alive and free. I made a promise to myself, that I would start thinking before I do some dirt because if I ever get cornered by the police, I'm holding court in the streets fuck going back to jail. Big Rome looked at Mark and shook his head in disappointment.

"Mark I been schooling you since you was a kid and you still a kid mentally. It's time for you to be a man. I'm tryna to leave the drug game alone and give you the throne, but you ain't even ready." Mark just sat there not saying nothing looking at the ground. Big Rome cell phone went off he answered it, said okay, and hung up. "Yo mama outside she said baby Mark want to stay with her. So I guess you free, I love you man. Mark tighten up. Ali, remember what I said," with that he grabbed his coat and left.

Mark got up walked right past me and went in his room. I thought about the two naked chicks in my bed and my dick jumped. I shrugged my shoulders and went to my room to get me a couple more nuts off.

JUMPING OFF
THE PORCH

Chapter 5

"Man, my pops be on bullshit cuz. He act like I need his ass to make money nigga, I'm my own man."

I can tell Mark was mad as fuck, so I just kept quiet and let him vent.

"He always doin that preaching shit, talking about rules. His ass don't know it's a young nigga world and young nigga don't follow rules, period." I sat and listened to mark as we rode around the hood on Fenkell. Mark pulled in the driveway of a two family flat on Monica and Chelfente. "Cuz, I know you ain't no nigga that just want hand outs and I respect that. If you really want to come up, we can do it together."

Now, he had my attention. "How, we gone do that Mark? You know I ain't no sport worker or nothing like that," I said in a serious tone.

"Naw, cuz just listen. It's a nigga from the east side name Cool who gettin a lot of money. I been fucking his baby mama for a minute. He got her ducked off over there on Puritan and Tuller," Mark told me as I past him the blunt.

"What make you think he got some cash in there cuz?"

"One day I spent the night over there and I fucked her ass to sleep, but I noticed she had a lot of expensive shit. So, I search around and found two safes. One in closet the other on her son's room in the wall behind a picture," Mark said.

"Okay, but if he a real street nigga then he ain't tell the bitch the combination. So, how imma get the safe open?"

"That's what I'm tryna tell you cuz. Every morning she used to make me leave before 8:00am. She walk her son to the school on the corner then Cool pulls up around 9:00 am on the nose."

"How you know what time he come if she put you out? Nigga, don't tell me you stalkin."

"I was curious cuz, so I had to check."

"Do yo pops do business wit the nigga?"

"Fuck Naw! My pops said back in the day him and the nigga Cool was beefin hard. All the blood shed had the police everywhere, so they ended up callin a truce, so they could get back to the money."

I sat there for a minute pondering on was it worth it or not. Then I said, fuck it! I ain't fin-da live off no nigga. "I'm wit it cuz."

"Hell yeah I knew you was my nigga. Let me introduce you to my young dog, real quick."

Me and Mark jumped out the car walked up to the side door and knocked on it the door opened and a lil nigga with long ass braids and tattoos everywhere came out. Under his right eye it said no fear.

"What's up my nigga? Mark, ain't seen yo ass in a minute."

"Shit bro, I been hustling my nigga stayin out the way," Mark said.

"I know ya'll nigga could come on in fool."

We came into the house and walked straight downstairs. It was guns everywhere. I almost came in my pants looking at all the weapons this nigga had.

"So, what's on yo mind Mark?"

"Big money as always. Damn I forgot, Ali this is my young dog Shy. He real as fuck and he wit the drama. He only 17 and got almost as many bodies as his age, you feel me?"

I nodded my head then he looked at Shy.

"Shy, this my cousin Ali. My nigga crazy as shit and he loyal."

Me and Shy shook hands and he passed me a blunt.

"Damn Mark, I heard about that shit you got into wit Twerk the other night," Shy said smiling.

"Yea, but I ain't trippin he ain't tryna see me, plus my pops straighten that shit out," Mark said.

Shy jumped off the couch and grabbed a Mini 14 with a drum on it. "Fuck them niggas Mark, you my nigga we can go slide on them niggas right now. You ain't even got to go just give me the word."

Now imma real nigga and I ain't no dick sucker, period. But, I ain't gone lie I like this young nigga style. He reminded me of myself in a lot of ways.

"Naw Shy, my pops said stand down, so that's what we gone do. But look that ain't why I came here. I got some shit on the floor, and I need you to get some shit for me."

Shy nodded his head, put the gun back on the shelf, and fired up another blunt.

"Okay my dog, just tell me what you need you know I got you."

"Look I'm fin-da put a play down on a nigga and I need you to get me a car. I want the car to be low-key, but fast just in-case." Shy nodded his head. "I also need a clean gun with two extra clips and a vest."

"Okay I got you Mark. I got the gun, the extra clips, and the vest come see tonight around midnight and I'll have the car for you, too."

As promised Shy had the car for us, it was a 2006 G6. It was small and low-key, but fast as shit. "So how much I owe you," Mark asked Shy.

"Fuck you just give me 1,000 and we good," Shy said. Yea I can tell he was a loyal nigga because niggas damn near paying 1,000 for the vest alone. Mark being the real nigga that he is gave him 2,000. Real niggas do real shit.

Mark showed me the house on Tuller. I stalked it out for a couple days, just to be on the safe side. Now I'm sitting two houses down from Cool's baby mama house. The G6 had tinted windows so that worked to my advantage, but the disadvantage was it was broad day light. Once I jumped out the car in all black imma look suspect if someone happen to see me especially, with the mask on. 8:00 on the dot I peeped chick coming out the house with a little boy. They walked right pass me and didn't even pay attention to me. The woman was too busy tellin her son if the school called her again, she was gone beat the black off him. I decided that it would be best to get her coming back from dropping her son off. I didn't want to have to hurt the lil nigga too. I made sure my 45 was locked and loaded, put my extra clips in my pocket just in case. I looked in my rearview window and noticed the chick coming back from the school. I leaned my seat all the way back and hit the unlock button on the car. I took a deep breath and hit my chest to remind myself that I was wearing a vest. The woman walked pass the car and I leaned my seat back up. I scanned the block one more time to make sure no one was outside this early, I was clear. She cut across the grass walking toward the porch. Before her feet touched the bottom step I was out the car on her ass. She didn't notice me until she was about to open the screen door. It was too late. I covered her mouth with my left hand, and I put the gun in her ribs with my right.

"Listen closely lil mama, this only a robbery won't turn it into a homicide, if I was gone kill you I wouldn't have worn a mask. I know Cool got a stash in here and I want it. If you bullshit me, imma kill you. I'm fin-da uncover yo mouth please don't scream, just unlock the door and let's go inside do you understand." She nodded her head yes.

"Is there anybody else in the house?" She shook her head no. She unlocked the door and we walked in the house. Once we got in the house, I found some Scotch tape and I taped her up. I looked at the clock on the wall, 8:45. I went around the house opening windows just in case shit went wrong and I have to do a quick escape. Once I heard the car pulling up in the driveway I got in position. I had the woman o the coach taped up in the fetal position like she was sleep. I put the cover over her so Cool wouldn't see the tape when he came in. I stepped in the closet by the front door but didn't close it. I left it cracked open so I could see Cool come through the door.

Cool came through the door. Damn! Mark didn't tell me how big and black this nigga was. "Shantae, wake yo ass up girl. Why the fuck you sleeping on the coach!" He bent down to kiss her, seen the tape on her mouth and his eyes got big as saucers. Before he had a chance to react, I was out the closet on his ass, 45 locked and loaded. I put the barrel behind his left ear and his whole body got stiff. "You betta kill me nigga, cause you ain't gettin shit."

I ain't gone lie, I respected this nigga gangsta. I feel like I would die for what I worked for too. But, as much as I respected that nigga gangsta, I respect mines a whole lot more. If I got to send this nigga to whatever higher power, he believed in then so be it. I hit his ass twice in back of the head hard as shit. Once I had him on the floor face down I cut his bitch tape off her hands then made her tape his ass up real good. Once that was done I punched his bitch in the nose as hard as I could. She hit the ground hard as fuck, her nose squirted out blood. I grabbed her by both her ankles and pulled her toward me. I re-taped her hands and feet and I put a pillowcase over her head. I don't know why I punched her, but I know it felt good. Seeing all that blood made the beast in me grow. Play time over back to business, I turned this fat fuck Cool on his back, took the tape off his mouth, and sat on his chest.

"Listen Cool, this how it's gone be I want all the money and dope you got in here and I want it now."

"I told you homie kill me. Naw cuz, I ain't given you shit." Damn this nigga had heart. I stood up and pulled his baby mama right on the side of him.

"We gone play a game Cool. It's real simple I asked a question, and you answer it truthfully. If I think you lying imma kill her right on the side of you. If you lie again, my mans outside gone kill yo son," I lied.

To put the icing on the cake, I pulled out my phone and pretended to call someone. "Aye, what up blood. Naw, he playin games. Look if I call you again go down to that school and kill that lil nigga, okay? You remember what he look like right? Okay bet," I lied. "Play time over Cool" I put the gun to his beaten head. "Question one. I know you got two safes one in yo baby mama closet, the other in yo son room behind a picture. What's the combination?" I looked Cool in the face, and I didn't see a drop of fear in his eyes. I took the pillowcase off his baby mama face; she was crying hard as fuck. I put the gun to her head and I looked at Cool. "What's the combination?" He still ain't say shit. Now I'm getting mad he must think imma pussy, okay bet. "I warned yo ass, but you think shit sweet." I went in my pants and grabbed a pocketknife I got from Shy. I flicked the knife out and I stabbed his bitch in the stomach five or six times, then I cut that bitches throat deep as fuck. Cool started to scream, so I taped his mouth up again. I grabbed a chair and just sat there watching this bitch die. I pulled out my phone and sat it on top of the dead bitch chest. "Imma ask you again what's the combinations?"

Now this muthafucka want to cooperate. I pick his big ass up and made him hop up the stairs. We went to his bitch room first. Once we got to the safe I put the gun to his head. "I promise you Cool if you try something slick imma blow yo shit off nigga. Just give me the money you can make it back, but if I kill you... well then you just fucked."

He seemed to ponder what I was saying then he opened the safe. I moved him out the way and found a bunch of neat stacks of money. Way more than I ever seen in my life. I grabbed a pillowcase and filled it up.

Next, I made his big ass hop to his son room. Once he moved the picture I noticed it was a bigger safe then the one in the women's room, way bigger. He opened the safe and my mouth dropped. Not only was there big stacks of money. It was five kilos of heroin too. I grabbed a big bag out the closet and put everything in it.

Cool looked at me crazy, "you know when I find you imma kill you."

I put the bag down and took off my mask, I looked him dead in his eyes before I blew his brains out. I hit him two more times before I left. I ran downstairs and shot baby mama twice in the head, NO WITNESSES!!!

CHAPTER 6

Mark and I sat at the table in the Livingroom counting big stacks of money. We had five bricks of heroin sitting in a Ladyboy chair, and when we were done counting the money we ended up with $250,000. That's 125 thousand a piece! Not bad for a nigga that just came home week and half ago. I was just about to ask Mark a question, when we heard a knock at the door.

Mark got up and opened the door and Big Rome came in and just stood there. Big Rome looked at the money on the table then at the bricks on the Ladyboy and shook his head.

"So ya'll the ones who lined up Cool, huh?" Neither one of us said anything, so he continued, "obviously, it was Mark's idea to put the play down because Ali don't know him. So, who's idea was it to call me?" Big Rome asked. Mark nodded his head toward me. "Why did you think it was smart to call me?"

"I only decided to call you because these bricks got a certain stamp on them. Mark told me that it's not the same stamp that's on yo work. Mark only deals with the clientele you handed down to him. So, more than likely it would've sent up red flags if the work was different and pointed the finger at us or you." I said this letting Big Rome I was a thinker, also.

"So, basically ya'll need me to sell'em."

"Hell yeah, but we can split the money," I told him.

He nodded his head up and down. "Good thinkin nephew, I don't approve of the move that ya'll pulled but as long as it don't come back to me I'm cool wit it," Big Rome said.

After that he gathered up the work and left. I looked at Mark and he had a big ass grin on his face.

"What the fuck you smiling at Mark?"

"It's time to go shoppin cuz."

"Auntie Pam got me enough shit to last until summer."

"Nigga fuck some clothes, we goin car shoppin. Unless you want to be a passenger, side nigga, your whole life," Mark teased me.

Mark knew exactly what to say to get me hype. Before I knew it we were in Mark's Audi truck on our way to get me my first car. Mark started playing a song that put me in the zone. "Damn who is this rappin cuz," I asked.

"This Future cuz, you better get hip."

We continued to ride while I bobbed my head *"We got blood on the money and we still count it."* A lot of people was scared of blood money, not me. I remembered the question I was about to ask Mark before Big Rome showed up so, I turned the radio down. "Aye cuz, you ain't worried about yo baby mama getting you set up, robbed, or something. She seem crazy as shit," I asked him.

Mark looked at me like I had two heads. "Hell Naw that bitch ain't that crazy Trust me, I was wit that hoe for four and half years cuz. She know all my spots and ain't hit one of them. She know the code to my safe that I stashed in her basement and the money ain't never short," Mark boasted. I nodded my head and left it alone.

Shortly after we pulled in a car lot right off 8 Mile and Prairie. We got out the truck and a short, fat, and bald man comes out to greet us.

"Mark, what's goin on buddy."

"Nothin much Burt, tryin to stay one step ahead of the Feds, you can relate to that can't you." Mark joked. Both of them laughed, but I didn't find shit funny so I just sat there.

"So what brings you to my lot today? You tired of the Audi already?"

"No actually, my cousin Ali right here, was hoping to find him something," Mark nodded toward me.

"Well Ali is it? If it's hot, I got it on my lot!" I guess that was his sales pitch, but he was right.

He had everything you could image, but only one really caught my eye. "Right here Burt, I want this one."

"Ahhhh, 2015 Jeep Cherokee straight. Good choice my friend," Burt said putting his hand on the back. I looked at his hand and he smartly removed it.

"So what's up Burt, tell me how much you

want for this?" Mark asked him getting right to business.

"Give me 75 thousand and it's all yours. I'll wright it up like you're leasing it for 85 hundred, you know keep the Feds off you and you will never have to pay a note." Mark nodded his head like it was good deal, so I went along with it but truthfully, I ain't never seen 75 thousand in my life. So, to spend it on a car with no hesitation felt a little surreal to me.

I drove of the lot in my new truck and I instantly fell in love with it. I followed Mark to some hole in wall car shop, more like a chop shop. Some Hispanic dude named Hector charged me 15 thousand for some all black Forgiato rims, a stash spot that made my whole dashboard lift-up and tinted my windows out. The stash spot was big enough to put a choppa in there, so I knew that was gone come in handy.

We pulled back up to Mark's crib and tried to figure out what was up for the night. I counted my stash it was a little over 35 thousand. Most people would have thought that was good, not me. I mean in my opinion; in some ways you are who you hang around. I know for a fact Big Rome has some millions put up and if by some chance Mark don't have at least a million put up, I know he has a couple hundred thousand. I ain't never been no runt of the crew, so I had to get my paper up.

Mark said, he had some hoes coming through. I was cool wit that, I was stalkin Cool so much, I ain't had no pussy since my first day off. About an

ANDRE CALVIN LEE JR

hour and half later, we heard the window then he unlocked the door. Mark started kissing one of the twins hard as shit. When they came up for air he looked at me. "Aye cuz, this my wife Desseray and this her twin Destiny. Ladies this my cousin Ali." I looked at Mark with a look that said, I thought Peaches was your wife. He smiled and shrugged his shoulders like hey, what can I do?

Both women were beautiful to say the least. Both of them looked like Cristina Millan, but way thicker. We chilled and talked and shit for a minute. Once everybody was drunk and high enough, they both went to separate bedrooms.

Once we got into my room Destiny stripped butt naked and laid on top of the bed. Her body was flawless. She had a tattoo of a snake starting at her ankle, wrapped around her leg all the way up into the inside of her thigh, with its mouth open like the snake was about to eat her pussy. "If you last 10 minutes, I'll be surprised," Destiny said.

What! I killed the rest of my cup, stripped naked then spread her legs. I looked at the clock 10:10 P.M. I put her ankles where her ears at and went to work on that pussy. 10 minutes my ass!!!

I woke up the next morning to a knock on the door.

"Nephew, let me holla at you." I looked at the clock 7:50 A.M. I wonder what the fuck Uncle Rome could want so early.

39

I looked at the sleeping beauty next to me and smiled. I fucked her for three and half long hours last night, till her pussy was sore and dry. I climbed out of the bed put on my shorts and walked to the Livingroom. Mark was already up eating some cereal and Uncle Rome was sitting in the Lazy boy. I sat down on the coach and fired up a half of blunt from the ashtray. "What up Unk?"

"Shit you tell me Nephew."

I know I had to have a confused look on my face. I turned to look at Mark and he just shook his head. What the fuck is going on?

"I see you got you a new car outside Neph. It look real expensive," Big Rome said.

"Yea Unk it cost a pretty penny but shit I can't ride in Marks' passenger side forever, just like I can't sleep in his guest bedroom forever. A man needs his own." I said.

Big Rome nodded his head like he understood. "So what's the two mistakes you made Ali?" Big Rome quizzed me I shrugged my shoulders because I didn't know. "First off, you spent a large lump sum of money without a guaranteed way to make it back. I mean it's easy to say you gone rob again, but how hard you think it's gone be to find somebody with that kind of money the beefing with?" I didn't know the answer so I kept quiet. "Secondly, any real hustla know that you never create to many bills for yo self. You got yo cell phone bill, car note, rent wardrobe, jewelry, trickin wit these lil hoes, and whatever other habits you got. What I'm sayin if you ain't got a consistent hustle don't ever create to many bills for yo self," Big Rome schooled us.

I'm starting to see why Big Rome has so much success in the drug game, he's smart. No matter what game you in if you listen and follow the rules more than not, you'll win. With that Big Rome reached on the side of the couch, grabbed a bag, and threw it at me. I unzipped it, looked in the side and my eyes popped out of my head.

"Damn Unk, what's this for?"

"I sold then bricks you gave me."

"Damn already?"

"Yea, my mans from Florida chopped them."

"He flew down here?"

"Naw, he was already here he on his way back now."

"Bet, let's split this shit up then."

"Naw nephew, that's all you. Mark got mo' money then he know what to do with and I don't need it so... welcome home."

I looked from Big Rome to Mark then at the money. "How much in here?"

"I sold all five of them for 90 thousand a piece. So that's 450 thousand Nephew."

Damn, I damn near expected the Feds to kick the front door in. I slapped fives with Mark and gave Big Rome a hug.

"Alright Nephew, go stash the gwop and come ride with me real fast I got to holla at you," Big Rome said.

I walked in my bedroom and noticed Destiny

still sound asleep. I quickly woke her ass up and made her get dressed and bounce. She had an attitude, but I ain't give a fuck. Mark was happy too, he made Desseray leave. I opened my closet reached up and pushed the attic door open. I stuffed the bag of money in there and closed it. I brushed my teeth put on the same clothes from yesterday then jumped in the truck with Big Rome. "What's up Unk," I asked as he took off down the road.

"I got somebody I want to introduce you to Nephew. My best friend and business partner, Tone."

"Stop me if I'm out of order Unk, but what I want to meet him for? That's yo mans."

"First off let me say, I trust Tone with my life so you can, too. I talked to him about the situation with Cool and he wanted to meet you, "Big Rome said.

"I'm still lost on why he want to meet me."

"Lately, a lot of people Tone been dealing with been shorting him on his cash and some people, just flat out not paying him. We had a nigga to handle shit like that, but that didn't work."

"What went wrong with the last nigga Unk?"

"The police picked him up for questioning and they tricked his dumb ass into a confession."

"Damn that's fucked up Unk. So, niggas playin with y'all paper and y'all want em gone, right?"

"Yea and No, see me and Tone a team but we got separate clientele. So really that's his money, but he still my mans."

"So, ya'll don't cop together," I asked.

"Yea and No again. See we got the same connect, but we both cop 15 kilos a piece at a time. I'm still coppin 15, lately Tone just been getting 10.

"Damn Unk, how you be flossin? I thought you was grabbin like 100."

"Naw Nephew. In real life, a nigga can live great going through one kilo of work, let alone 15." I guess he was right.

I noticed we was in the hood once I started seeing all of the vacant houses. We pulled up to a house on the corner of Stoepel and Chalfante and parked. Big Rome jumped out the car so, I followed suit. We walked through a gate and walked around to the back of the house. I saw a short fat man with a full beard in the back yard. He had a whole lot of grey hair and he was feeding no less than nine pit bulls. He had a full jumpsuit like he worked on cars and dirty hands. This can't be Tone. He looked up at us, smiled, and came our way to greet us.

"Rome, what's up boss?" They shook hands. He looked at me, "You must be Ali? It's nice to meet you son. I heard a lot about you." I don't if it was because he's dirty or what, but I got a bad vibe from him. "Look Ali, I'm sure Rome told you why I need you, so let me know how you feel about that."

I looked at Big Rome he nodded his head at me. "Long as the paper straight I'll kill anybody," I said seriously.

Big Rome and Tone started laughing, but neither of them knew how serious I really was. Big Rome got serious and looked at me. "Nephew, Tone family and in this game family takes care of family. Always remember, one hand wash the other and both hands wash the face." We rode back to Mark's house in silence. Big Rome got a phone call and turned the music up some, so I wouldn't be able be able to hear his conversation. I smiled to myself; hey I guess that's how you stay free by staying cautious. When we pulled up to Mark's house, I noticed Auntie Pam car was there. Big Rome and I climbed out his truck and walked toward the door. It was unlocked.

"Boy if I ever hear about you putting yo hands on a woman, imma kill you Mark," Auntie Pam yelled.

"Ma, she out of order! How she got a nigga around my son like that?" They both looked up and noticed us and stopped the whole conversation.

Big Rome looked at his wife then his son and shook his head. "I don't want to know anyway," he said then continued. "Look Mark go grab me a half of brick fast, so I can bump into my mans real fast. I'll replace the work for you when I came back out here tonight," Big Rome said.

Mark looked at Big Rome and shook his head. "Naw pops let me make the sale. You said you tryna retire. I might as well start meetin wit yo clientele," Mark said.

"Naw maybe next time mark."

Mark shook his head and Auntie Pam spoke up for him.

"Let that boy gone head bae, I need to get my car detailed anyway. It take 24 hours so, you gone have to take me home."

Big Rome thought for a minute then said fuck it. "Mark, you goin to meet my dog Pooh. He from Linwood so I charge him 50 thousand for a half brick of heroin, you got that?"

"Yea, I got it Pops. Where do he want me to meet him at?" Mark asked.

Big Rome looked at Mark like he was the stupidest person alive. "How many times I got to tell you Mark, you the one with the work. You don't never let no nigga tell you where he want you to go because then he can set up an ambush on his terms. You got to always set the meeting location that way the advantage works in your favor," Big Rome schooled.

Mark nodded his head to the game then asked, "fuck it, can Ali ride with me Pops?"

Again, he shook his head, "what I tell you about business Mark?" Mark had a blank look on his face. "No offense Ali, but if a person is not directly involved in the business don't involve them. The less people know, the better."

That's cool I thought, I needed a nap anyway. I walked in my room undressed, laid down, maybe take a quick three-hour nap and with that I was gone.

Juice sat at the Dining room table smoking a fat ass Backwood full of Granddaddy Kush. He looked down at the sexy ass slut devouring his whole dick. Juice was the shit and he knew it. Juice was about 5'10, 175 pounds, light skin, grey eyes, with a head full of 360's. He looked over at his twin brother Tommy. Him and Tommy were like night and day. Even though they looked alike Tommy was younger by like 12 minutes. Instead of waves Tommy had dreadlocks that hung down to his shoulders. Juice was a ladies' man, but Tommy was the devil with grey eyes.

Tommy loved killing more than pussy and everybody knew that. Juice smiled then looked at Bay Boy. Bay Boy was a short brown skin dude with tattoos over his whole body, including face. His hair stayed nappy and he had a voice that annoyed everybody.

Juice heard a cell phone go off and turned to look at Gutta the oldest out the bunch. Gutta was black as shit with a bald head and full beard. He rarely ever smiled, but he was the leader. Gutta was 23, Bay Boy was 19, Juice and Tommy were both 17. What did they have in common? All them were stone cold killers. They killed for money, respect, reputation, and for fun. Each one of them got the letters C.B.K. tatted on them, which stood for "Cold Blooded Killas." He heard Gutta tell whoever was on the phone that we wanted half up front and half later, like every other time. He knew that meant they had a job to do which meant some more money. That made his dick even harder. Juice looked down at Keisha sexy ass sucking the shit out his dick. He grabbed her by her dreadlocks and pushed her head down making her swallow his kids. That bitch ain't waste a drop.

Mark was riding down Fenkell smoking on a Kush blunt feeling like the shit. Regardless to what his pop's said Mark knew he was made for this shit. The money, the bitches, the clothes, and the cars. That's what he lived for. Mark looked at his 60-thousand-dollar *Rolex* watch and noticed he was late. Shit, he told Pooh to meet him at the store on Fenkell and Greenlawn, that was 20 minutes ago. Fuck it, Mark figured that as long as he met Pooh in his own hood he didn't have to worry about getting set up. He turned in the parking lot and it was empty. What the fuck?

He pulled his IPhone and called Pooh. "Damn fool, where you at?"

"I'm pullin in now bro."

"Okay, bet."

Juice, Tommy, and Gutta loaded the Draco choppas they had in the back of a stolen Caravan. Bay Boy was the best driver so; he was behind the wheel. Gutta phone rung he said okay and hung up. He didn't even have to say anything.

All three of them jumped out the van, which was parked on the side of the store. They all pulled their mask down and jogged around the store. Gutta peeked around the corner and didn't see the long sleeve Caddy truck that was supposed to be there. What the fuck, only car in the parking lot was an Audi truck. Fuck it, niggas getting money switch cars all the time. All three of them slid from around the corner and opened fire on the Audi truck **BOC! BOC! BOC! BOC! BOC! BOC! BOC!**

Juice, Tommy, and Gutta all had 30 round clips and they didn't stop shooting until they were empty. Then they ran jumped in the car so Bay Boy can get them a clean get-a-way. Once they were far away they pulled in an alley, they had a gas can full of gasoline. They soaked the car then set it on fire. They jumped another fence to an abandon house, where they had another get-a-way car stashed. They took the clips out the choppas and put the guns and clips in big black bags once they made it to their next destination. They would bury the guns 3 feet deep, like they always did and no one will ever find them.

CHAPTER 7

We had Marks funeral on Pennbroke and Livernois, at the New Prospect Baptist Church. It was so crowded a lot of people had to stand outside until it was time to alternate with people inside. I stood in the back of the church the whole time and my heart broke with every passing second. Mark was shot so many times with 7.62 bullets that an open casket was out of the question. I looked at Big Rome and my Auntie Pam both crying their hearts out. Big Rome was broken up because he knew the hit was for him. Auntie Pam was just as crushed because she had been the one who pushed Big Rome to let Mark go make the sale. Next to them Big Rome's right-hand man, Tone, was there also. He was crying just as hard as them, even though I had a bad feeling about him. It didn't take a rocket scientist to see that he had a lot of love for Mark and that by itself made me like him a little bit more. Just a little bit though! Mark's baby mother Keisha was also there holding Baby Mark, both of them were crying hysterically.

Now I was getting pissed off. I needed blood and I needed it fast. As I turned to leave I bumped into a woman, I was about to spazz out but, when I looked into her face it was the most beautiful face I ever saw. I lost my breath.

"I'm so sorry Ali, I wasn't even paying attention. Sorry for your loss," the pretty woman said to me.

I was about to respond, but then I realized that she just called me by my name. "Utt, sorry but do I know you from somewhere."

"Oh my God, you don't remember me? I know I lost a lot of weight but damn," she faked an attitude.

As soon as she said that it came to me. "Wow, Trina is that you," I asked.

"Yea people call me Red now, but yea it's me."

I noticed she had red hair, hints the name. I did a full body look over and she had a body to die for. Nice plump ass and perfect C cup breast. About time I made it back up to her face, I noticed she was giving me the same once over. We both smiled and looked away embarrassed. I looked toward Mark's casket and instantly felt guilty about flirting at his funeral.

"Well, it was nice seeing you again Ali. Don't be a stranger and again I'm sorry for yo loss," with that she walked off.

I couldn't help but stare at her ass. She approached a short dude with braids and they talked for a second. Once he turned around I noticed that it was Shy, the young savage that Mark introduced me to with all the guns. When he noticed me he walked straight toward me.

"What up Ali? Man, sorry for yo loss God. You

know imma ride just give the word." Shy lift his shirt up and showed me a 40 Cal. I knew I liked this kid. I showed him the 45 I had in a holster inside my tux. "Aye God, check it. That bitch ass nigga Pooh hiding out real good, but I got a feeling that pussy gone poke his head out sooner or later. But right now, I got the next best thing," Shy said. My ears perked up now, everybody been looking for this nigga Pooh. Big Rome even put 100,000 on the nigga head but, still can't nobody find him. So, when Shy brought his name up you can see why I got interested. "I did some homework and I found out that nigga moms stay on Puritan and Wyoming. She stay on Indiana St. between Mary Groove and Florence."

"Okay, you got the address?"

"Yea God. Here, I wrote it down for you."

"Hell yea, I appreciate it Shy. Imma make sho my uncle know you helped. So he can put some money in yo pocket."

Shy frowned his face, "Naw God, you got the wrong idea. Mark was my nigga fuck that money; nigga pay me in blood."

I told him I would keep that in mind, but we both knew I was lying. I mean I liked Shy he seemed 100, but I didn't know him nor did I trust him enough to body some shit in front of him. But, just to keep it G wit him I told him to meet me at his crib in an hour so I can buy some more guns. I didn't really have a plan. I was just moving off emotion now, which is bad and that's what scared me. But, one thing I did know is, imma kill every single person I think I was involved, PERIOD!!!

I sat two houses down from Pooh's mother house. I been sitting in a stolen Impala for three and a half hours. After I went to Shy's to buy some guns I paid him to get me a car, also. I was about to fire up another blunt when I saw the front door open. An older heavy-set woman came out with two trash bags in her hand. I jumped out the car and walked up to her.

"Excuse me ma'am, let me help you with them bags," I asked politely.

"Oh thank-you young man. Bad as my knees are I need to be lying down."

"Don't mention it. Here let me help you up the stairs."

"God bless you, young man. A lot of young people today don't have manners."

This shit was too easy. I helped her in the house and sat her down in a rocking chair. She told me thank-you again and turned around like I was leaving. Instead I closed the front door and turned around with my gun out. She put her hands to her mouth like she was surprised and started praying. I pulled a chair up directly in front of her. Then without warning I slapped the shit out of her as I could. **WACK!**

"Listen bitch, I'm lookin for your son Pooh. I will not hesitate to kill you in order to find him. Now, do you know where he is?" She shook her head no, so I slapped her again. **WACK!** "I'm going to kill him anyway. You're only slowing down the inevitable."

"Young man, God bless your soul."

I looked around the room and I saw a bunch of crosses and pictures of Jesus with Bible scriptures next to them. I realized this woman wasn't going to give up her son because she believed that she was going to Heaven. I got mad then but, this time I punched the shit out of her and she flipped out the rocking chair. Her eye was swelling up real fast but, instead of telling me what I wanted to know she crawled to her knees and started praying again.

"Heavenly father, though I walk..." **BOC! BOC!** I shut that shit up instantly. Mk 45 opened her head up easily. Her wig flew off and for some strange reasoned I found that funny, so I laughed. I kicked her in the stomach for no reason at all and I began to ransack the house.

I heard a car pulling in the driveway so I ran to the window. A dark skin woman jumped out of a grey Trailblazer and walked up to the door. I heard her key go in the door so, I stood behind it. Once she opened the door she saw the old woman on the ground and she ran to her. I came up behind her and clocked her with my 45., she passed out. I carried her up to a bedroom and I tied her hands and feet to the bed frame, so it looked like she was making a snow angel. Then I taped her mouth and splashed cold water on her, she woke up instantly.

"Wake up sleepy head," I mocked her. She

looked very scared. "Look, I'm looking for Pooh do you know him?" She nodded her head yes, so far so good. "Okay, good. I'm going to kill him because he killed somebody close to me. Now the old lady she chose not to tell me where he was and... well you see how that turned out," she nodded again. "Alright now, before I ask you the same question, I'm going to show you why you shouldn't lie to me." Her eyes got wide as fuck.

I pulled out a cigar cutter and I chopped off five of her toes. She passed out after the second one. I splashed her again and she woke up instantly.

"Now that we understand each other do you know where pooh is?" She nodded her head yes, "Good answer."

After I got rid of the car, the clothes, and my 45. I jumped in another hot car, with another 45, and as usual all black. I was about to go kill Pooh but, I wanted to holla at Big Rome first so I called him.

"Aye Unk, I got a location on that one nigga I'm on my way to see him now."

"Okay Nephew, keep me posted." I heard someone in the background ask Big Rome a question and he told him what I said. Had to be Tone, Big Rome came back to the phone. "Aye Nephew, you did good but, I need to holla at you. You know these phones ain't no good. So, pull up on me real quick."

"Where you at Unk?"

"I'm at the bat cave."

"Okay, I'm on my way." I did a U-turn and drove toward the bat cave, which was a hideout for Big Rome.

I got to the bat cave 30 minutes later and I pulled around back. The bat cave was just an old barber shop on Plymouth and Evergreen that Big Rome and Tone had meetings and stashed dope. Big Rome let me through the back and we embraced.

"We missed you at the grave site Nephew."

"Yea Unk you know I couldn't handle that."

"I know Nephew, I know."

We walked in and I saw Tone sitting at a table on the phone. When he noticed us he hung up then stood up.

"Ali, what's good fam? You okay?"

I just nodded my head then sat down. Big Rome asked me what happen at Pooh's mother house. I looked at Tone one more time then I explained the situation from start to finish.

"You sure she gave you the right info," Tone asked.

"Yea, I'm pretty sure."

"Damn you a cold blooded muthafucka, Ali. You wacked the mama and sista," Tone said.

I didn't respond I just looked I just looked right in his eyes trying to see if I saw anything, flaw in his soul, lucky for him his cell phone went off.

He looked down at the phone. "Aye, I gotta take this call Rome," Tone said and he jumped up and went toward the front.

Big Rome read my mind. "Nephew Tone good

people. I trust him with my life."

"Yea, I hear you Unk."

"Anyway, me and yo Auntie goin out of town for a couple days. Get our heads togetha real quick."

"Yea, ya'll need to Unk."

"I know. Imma leave all my business in Tones hands while I'm gone."

"Cool and imma be making the streets bleed till I feel better," I said seriously."

He smiled at that, "I love you Neph."

"I love you too, Unk. Let me get up out of here, so I can go get this nigga Pooh."

"Okay and Neph, don't just kill'em get some info."

"What you mean Unk?"

"He just a pawn Nephew. Somebody put him on me and that's who I want." He was right I wasn't even lookin at it like that. I was just gone kill Pooh's ass.

I went back on my journey towards the eastside where Pooh was hiding out at, all the way there I thought about Mark. My blood was boiling and I looked forward to torturing Pooh. I pulled up to an apartment building on Margaret and Chariton. I cocked my 45 put it in my pants and jumped out the car. When I got to the door I realized you need a key or somebody had to buzz you in, SHIT! I was about to just start buzzing random apartments until someone buzzed me in or so I thought, until I noticed two light skin guys quickly coming down the stairs. One had braids the other had a haircut, once I looked I realized they were twins. They came out the apartment and a minivan pulled up with two more guys in it. They jumped in and pulled off.

As I made my way up to the third floor I pulled the mask over my face to hide my identity. Once I got to the third floor I walked to #11 and the door was open just a little bit. I pulled my strap out and walked inside. At first glance the place looked regular, like someone left but didn't close the door all the way. I checked the Livingroom, the Kitchen, and the bedroom. All empty. I was about to leave, but I to piss. I opened the bathroom door and what do I see? Pooh. I shook my head and thought about the two niggas I saw coming out the building. It wasn't a fasho way for me to know if they came out of this apartment. But what I did know is whoever was here tied Pooh up, beat the shit out of him, drowned him in the tub, and then shot him for good measure. Just like I planned to do.

Now I was back at square one, I walked out the apartment confused and pissed off. I had my suspicion on what happened but, no proof. I ditched the car and made my way home. I fell asleep in deep thought.

CHAPTER 8

I sat on the couch at Mark's house smoking a blunt in deep thought. I couldn't believe somebody had beat me to Pooh. Somebody was obviously covering their tracks, but who? I leaned my head back and looked at the ceiling and something occurred to me, Twerk. Mark got into it with him at the club. I remember Big Rome saying he wasn't small time, so Twerk was working with some money. Mark wasn't the intended target, maybe Twerk planned on killing Big Rome first so he can eventually kill Mark anyway. I'm not sure though, too many loopholes. How would I get in touch with Twerk, anyway? I didn't want to go through Big Rome because I wasn't because I wasn't 100% sure it was Twerk. Then it came to me, Peaches! That's what Mark and Twerk got into it about in the first place. Yea, I can catch her at the club and make her talk. I looked at the clock 10:35 P.M. I grabbed a baby 40 out my closet jumped in my truck and headed toward Silver-Rain.

When I pulled up to Silver-Rain I saw the same bouncer from the last time. I just hope he still remembers my face. I peel 5 hundred dollar bills off my knot then folded them in my hand. I approached

ANDRE CALVIN LEE JR

the bouncer, and when he noticed me he put his hand out for a five. Yes! I passed him the money and he pulled me in for hug.

"Aye, man sorry for yo loss. Mark was like my people, too."

I just nodded my head as I walked into the bar. No need to respond I didn't see him at the funeral, so fuck him. I walked through the club watching everything; niggas throwing money, bad bitches naked. I didn't see peaches but, one thing prison has taught me is patience. A pretty ass brown skin stripper approached me after a minute or so.

"Hey daddy can you buy me a drink?"

"I can buy you more than that, if you worth it."

"Okay big money, you went to go to the Champagne Room."

"Yea, with Peaches."

She rolled her eyes and turned to walk away but, I grabbed her arm. She snatched away from me. "Hold on little mama slow down. I got $300 you point me in the right direction." I noticed some of her attitude melt away then.

"Make it $500 and I'll do more than that."

I pulled out some money and her whole face lit up. I gave her the money and her whole face lit up. I gave her the money and she turned around and left. A minute later Peaches came out the back walking in my direction. Damn she was still sexy as fuck.

"You looking for me?"

"Yea."

"Sorry about Mark. I didn't come to the funeral because I couldn't see him like that. You know?" I didn't say a word. Once she noticed I wasn't going to respond she continued, "Sooo, what's up Ali. I know you ain't come this far to stare at me."

"Actually, I did but I do plan to do more, than just stare at you."

She raised her eyebrows then put on a sexy ass smile. "You sure you ready for that, Mr. Ali?"

As much as I wanted to spit in this hoe face, I smiled my pretty boy and winked my eye. "What time you get off?"

"Whatever time you tell me to get dresses daddy."

I'm not gone lie I see why Mark was fuckin this bitch. She had too much sex appeal. Like the boss I am I told that bitch to "hurry up" and she went to the back to get dressed.

Fifteen minutes later, we was walking out the bar jumping in my truck. "I like yo truck," Peaches said to me.

I fired up a blunt passed it to her, then I fishtailed out the parking lot. We pulled into a cheap motel on 8 Mile and Woodward called the Motorama Motel. I made her go pay, so my face wouldn't be on the camera. She came out flashing me the keys, so I got out the car and followed her to our room. Once we into the room my plan was to start beating information out of her, but she through me off when she started stripping naked. Damn!

Peaches had to be the thickest woman I ever

laid eyes on. She bent over and started clapping her ass showing me her pussy. My dick got hard as Chinese arithmetic. She turned around, walked toward me, pushed me against the door and dropped to her knees. She wrestled with my Gucci belt for a second, undid my zipper and pulled my dick out. She started sucking my dick real fast and sloppy; I'm talking about real sloppy! She was using two hands and a whole lot of spit. She took my dick out her mouth then started licking up and down my shaft, then she jumped up, climbed on the bed, and got on all fours.

I damn near ran to the bed to dive in that pussy. I started off moving slow so we can catch our rhythm.

"Ooohhh, that feel good as fuck." As soon as she said that I turnt up on her ass.

"Oh that feel good, huh? I must be doin something wrong then!" I smacked her ass hard as fuck and started pounding that pussy out. She started screaming loud and throwing that ass back so hard, that I ended up coming faster than I intended to but fuck it. We both was breathing hard as shit.

"Come on lil mama, let's go jump in the shower togetha." I fucked her one more time in the shower and then we both washed up. Once I was satisfied that we were both clean, I told her to turn the water off. I put her ass in a choke hold. She tried to struggle but after about 25 seconds, she passed out.

She woke up, I had her legs and feet tied, and her mouth duck taped. She was still in the tub naked. "Look Peaches, imma say this once and one time only. I want Twerk. I been killin hoes all week don't become a statistic." She started nodding her head up and down real fast. I walked out the bathroom and came back in with her phone. "Do you know where Twerk stay at?" again with nodding her head fast. I cut off the tape on her hands then removed the tape off her mouth. "I don't care what you have to do or what you have to say, but you better call Twerk and make him invite you to his house, and you better do it fast."

I sat in a stolen car a few doors down from where Twerk stayed at. He had a modest house on Fielding and Tyreman. Peaches been in there for about 20 minutes. I'm waiting for her to give me the sign. My phone beeped letting me know I had a text. I looked at it and seen one word "open."

I got out the car and walked around to the side of the house looking for the bathroom window. Once I found it I pushed it up before I could climb through it I felt cold steal being put to the back of my head. Damn! I guess I should have expected the bitch to double cross me, huh?

"Nigga lay down on yo stomach. If you move crazy imma slump yo bitch ass." This nigga voice sounded familiar.

I got to try and buy some time, so I can get the

upper hand. "Look Homie, if you gone kill me, you gone have to kill me on my feet. I'm not getting on my stomach."

"Oh you think I'm playin, huh God?" He clicked the hammer back and I closed my eyes. Wait a minute did he just call me God?

"Shy is that you?"

"Oh shit Ali, I almost bodied yo ass God. What the fuck you doin here?" Shy asked.

"Shit I'm fin-da kill this nigga Twerk. I ain't know you work for this nigga, Shy."

"Work for him? Naw, I'm here to rob his ass. You know this nigga got the bag?"

"Yea, I think he got something to do with Mark."

"Damn, ok so what's next you know he got a bitch in there right?"

"Yea I know. How you think I got the bathroom window open?" We laughed for a second then got back to business.

"Look, we both might as well go in. We both kill'em and we both split the money," Shy said.

I was cool with that, since Shy was shorter than me he climbed through the window first. I passed him his 21 short 9mm and my baby 40 Cal., then I climbed in last. It wasn't hard to find what room they were in; we just followed the moans.

Once we got to the door I pushed it open slowly. Twerk was laying on his back while Peaches road the shit out of him, Me and Shy walked in the room unnoticed. Pussy was every weak nigga down fall. I grabbed Peaches by the back of the hair and yanked her off of Twerk hard as fuck. His eyes got wide as shit when he noticed me and Shy both standing there with guns in our hands.

"Aye man, what ya'll doin? Lil Shy what's goin on man?" Twerk was shaking like a muthafucka.

"I think you know why we here pussy! You thought you was just gone set Mark up to get killed and not have to pay," I said to Twerk.

He looked confused, "what, I didn't have nothing to do with that. Why would I do that? "I looked at him with a look that said nigga you know why.

"Aw man, Peaches! Fuck Naw, she just a hoe with good pussy."

"You tried to kill Big Rome so you can kill Mark later, but you lucked up and got Mark first."

"Why would I kill Big Rome, man? That's who I get all my work from."

He was right though; I feel like I'm a pretty good judge of character and I feel like Twerk was telling the truth. I looked at Shy and nodded.

Shy looked at Twerk without saying shit for about a full 60 seconds. I can tell it was making Twerk even more uncomfortable. "Look Twerk, you know I do my homework and you know I do it good. Tell me where the work and money at. Since you ain't have shit to do with mark we don't have to kill you, but if you lie…"

Twerk told him to go downstairs and move the deep freezer and there was a trap door under

64

there. He gave him the key and Shy went to go get the money. Fifteen minutes later, Shy walked in the room right pass me and shot Twerk in the head 3 times. **BOC! BOC! BOC!**

"Damn! What, he was lyin?" I asked.

"Hell Naw! I got that shit, but me and yo both know he was dead anyway for seeing our face. I smiled because he was right. I knew Shy was a real nigga.

"Now, let's whack this bitch and get the on," Shy said.

Fuck! I turned around and ran through the house looking for Peaches while Ali did the same thing. We were both so focused on Twerk, that we let Peaches get away from the scene. This was bad. I knew we wouldn't catch her at the club no more. We have to find her ass fast, or we bout to be in trouble.

Keisha sat on the toilet in the bathroom nervous as fuck. She kept bouncing her leg impatiently, holding the stick waiting for an answer. Two blue lines appeared. Fuck fuck fuck, she thought. How could I get pregnant by this nigga? Keisha pondered about should she tell Juice, whether or not she was pregnant. Then she thought fuck it, why not? She walked out the bathroom and approached Juice's room door. When she heard him whispering on the phone, being the jealous person that she was; Keisha put her ear to the door to hear more.

"So what, he still want us to whack Big Rome or no?" Juice asked whoever was on the phone with. "Bro. it's not our fault that we got Mark! He was at the wrong place, wrong time. He laughed and continued to talk shit.

Keisha walked back to the bathroom, flushed the toilet, and walked to the door like she just used the bathroom. Juice ended the phone call laid back in the bed and pulled his dick out. Like an obedient woman Keisha did what she was suppose too, in deep thought the whole time.

The next day me and Shy looked up and down for Peaches with no luck. Last night we looked $350,000 from Twerk and 3 pounds of Kush. We split everything down the middle. Our first priority was to find Peaches. Once word got out that Twerk was dead, the only person that could point us out was Peaches. We pulled in a Coney Island on 7 Mile and John R to get something to eat.

When my phone went off, I didn't know the number. "Who this," I said.

"This Keisha, Mark baby mama."

"I remember you what's up?"

"I know who killed Mark. I don't want to talk on the phone come to my house."

"Okay, shoot me the address."

"Okay and Ali, come by yo self." With that she hung up the phone.

A few minutes later I got a text. I put the

address in the navigational system and me and Shy shot out to Keisha's crib on 6 Mile and Telegraph.

"Look Shy, stay in the car. If I ain't out in 20 minutes come in guns blazing." Shy told me he would and I believed him.

I got out the car and I instantly saw a bunch of dogs on the side of the house barking. At least five of them behind the fence. I walked to the front door and knocked. It was an air conditioner in the front window and it was on. I knocked harder.

"Here I come, damn," Keisha shouted. She opened the door with nothing but a towel on. "Sorry Ali, I was in the shower." I followed her in the house to the bedroom and she sat down and started putting on lotion.

"So what's up, you got something to tell me?" with that Keisha told me everything she heard from beginning to end. I was getting madder and madder as she talked. "Okay good, and you sure that's what you heard?"

"Yea, Positive."

"Okay bet, I got something for his ass. Let me go grab Shy real fast so you can tell him what you told me," I said but, she stopped me.

"Hold on Ali, word on the street is you a shooter."

"What's yo point Keisha?" I asked.

She took the towel off and started playing with her pussy fast as shit. "I was just asking because imma shooter, too." I turned around and walked the fuck out of there.

I mean Keisha was bad and my dick was hard as fuck, but Mark was my cousin and you got to draw the line somewhere. Obviously, she didn't know that.

Once Keisha was dressed, she told Shy what she told me.

"Okay Ali, I got good news and bad news," Shy said. "The good news is, I know the niggas she talkin bout. The bad news is, them muthafuckas just as crazy as you."

Shy started tellin me about the four dudes that were in a gang called C.B.K. He described them to me and I got pissed.

"Fuck! I'm almost positive that them was the twins I saw coming out of Pooh's building," I said.

"So what you want to do God? You know whatever it is I'm with it," Shy said.

"You know where they stay at," I asked.

"Naw, but I know where they hang a lot."

"Good. I got a plan then." I looked at Keisha and she frowned her face up.

"What?"

"I need you to call Juice."

"Why?" I gave her a look that I'm pretty sure scared the fuck out of her. "Okay, Damn!"

I moved my truck down the street from Keisha's house in the driveway of an abandoned house. Me and Shy sat on the couch in the Livingroom while Keisha was at the kitchen table, snorting lines of coke.

"Take it easy on that shit, I need you to act natural. Not all high and jittery."

"Fuck you Ali. I'm nervous as shit them boys crazy," before I could respond a car pulled up in the driveway.

"Okay he here, Keisha."

Me and Shy both hid in the closet by the front door.

Keisha open the door and Juice came in and kissed her. "What's so important that you can't tell me on the phone, Keisha?" Juice asked.

"I don't know how to tell you this, but I know two people who want to kill you."

"What! Who?" Me and Shy came out the closet and put our guns to Juice head at the same time.

"Us, muthafucka. Now turn around."

Juice had his hands in the air, he pointed at Keisha and said, "Bitch you know you dead right?" He didn't wait for a response he turned toward us, "and what the fuck you two pussy niggas want, C.B.K. ain't taking no more initiations," Juice said with a smile.

Shy punched him in his mouth hard as fuck and he fell. I put my foot on his chest, while Shy searched and took his pistol.

"Damn Shy, you hit like a bitch," Juice said.

I was gettin pissed at his arrogance. "Look fool, you want to save yo self? Just tell me who put you on Big Rome," I asked.

"Nigga I ain't tellin you shit. Fuck Big Rome,

fuck you, fuck him, fuck this bitch, and fuck Mark. How bout that," Juice spat.

Shy pulled a double barrel shot gun out his pants and put it to Juice's head. "Now, I'm getting pissed Juice. Tell us what we want to hear or die," Shy said.

Juice put his hands behind his head and crossed his feet like he was getting a tan on the beach. "I said fuck you pussy. How many times I gotta-**BOOM!**

Shy knocked half of Juices head off. Keisha ran in the Kitchen and started throwing up.

"Damn Shy, yo trigger happy ass. We could've tortured him," I said.

"Naw God, he wasn't gone neva talk, trust me!!"

After we calmed Keisha down and cleaned up the mess. Me and Shy put Juice's body in the back of my truck. We debated back and forth on rather we should kill Keisha or not. We both decided that it would be stupid not to kill her, but because of our love for Mark neither one of us wanted to be the ones that did it. So, we set off on our journey.

We pulled up to a house on Fenkell and Washburn; he second house off the corner. We were parked in the middle of the street. I hit a button and the rear door opened up. Shy rolled Juice's body out the back onto the street.

"You ready?" I asked Shy. He nodded his head.

Shy grabbed a A.R. with 100 round drum on it and I grabbed the choppa with the 100-round drum, we both entered a round into the chamber. We both let off 100 shots at the hangout spot of the C.B.K. clowns. When were done the house could barely stand. We left Juice's body in the street with no head on it. They fucked up when they killed my cousin, but it's cool. Imma make the streets rain blood until I'm satisfied.

CHAPTER 9

Tommy, Bay Boy, and Gutta sat in a stolen minivan a few houses down from their intended target. They weren't home when their house got shot up, but they pulled up 10 minutes later. Tommy cried like a bitch when he saw his other half headless in the streets. The C.B.K. tattoo on his body left no doubt in their mind who it was. Truthfully, they had so much beef it was impossible to say who killed Juice. But, the last thing Juice said to Tommy was he was going to Keisha's house. So whatever happened from then till now, she knew about it. He told Juice several times after they killed Mark to leave Keisha alone, but Juice moved to his own beat and there wasn't a living soul that could change that.

So now, they were sitting on Keisha's block trying to figure out the best way to get it. Bay Boy hit the blunt and passed it back to Tommy. A grey Pacific truck pulled in Keisha's driveway and hit the horn. Keisha came outside, walked up to the car, and opened the back door. She pulled a little boy out the car seat and said goodbye to the driver. She carried the little boy in the house and closed the door.

After another 20 minutes of sitting there, they decided to make their move. Bay Boy started the car but left the head lights off. They pulled in the driveway and Tommy and Gutta got out the car as quietly as they could. As soon as the car door closed the dogs on the side of the house began to bark. They made their way to the front door and tried it, but it was locked. Tommy put his ear to the door but couldn't hear anything because of the air conditioning. Gutta and Tommy both looked at each other and nodded their heads. Tommy lifted the window while Gutta hung on to the air conditioning. Once the window was up Tommy helped Gutta lift the A.C. out the window and sat it down quietly. First Tommy climbed through the window followed by Gutta.

They could hear Keisha's voice in the back. "No boy, lay yo ass down you not getting nothin to drink, fuck around and piss on yo self." Tommy and Gutta followed Keisha's voice to the room she was in. Baby Mark waved at Tommy which mad Keisha turn around. Before Keisha could say anything Tommy grabbed her by her throat and dragged her out of her son's room. Gutta picked up Baby Mark in a non-threating way and followed Tommy to the Livingroom.

"Bitch you set my brother up."

"No I didn't Tommy I swear to God I didn't have a choice. They made me," Keisha cried.

"Who made you bitch? If you lie imma kill yo dusty ass."

Keisha began to tell Tommy everything that happened from the time they showed up to her house and left. She left out the part about hearing Juice on the phone and calling Ali over to tell him.

"Oh Yea, so Lil Shy and Mark's cousin did this huh? Why would they assume we killed Mark?"

"Ali said he saw you and Juice coming out the building Pooh's body was found in. So he put two and two together," Keisha lied.

When Tommy was satisfied, he choked the life out Keisha. Tommy stared in her eyes the whole time till she died. Then Tommy grabbed Baby Mark from Gutta, he grabbed him a Capri Sun out of the fridge. He walked over to the kitchen sink and opened the window above it. He stuck his head out and whistled. All five dogs ran to the window and started barking at Tommy. Tommy smiled and threw Baby Mark out the window. With that him and Gutta left without saying a word.

I was on the block sitting in the new Jaguar with Big Rome. Ever since Mark died he's been switching cars every week.

"Man Nephew, all this blood shed because of me. I feel fucked up man."

"If that's the case I'm just as guilty as you. I'm the one who been applying pressure on these niggas Unk."

"Damn, why they have to kill Lil Mark?"

I didn't say anything because I didn't think Big Rome wanted to hear the truth. Only a killa knows how a killa thinks and I knew firsthand why they killed Lil Mar; just to send a message.

"I see you got you a new truck Nephew."

"Yea, Silverado pick-up truck."

"I see you been with Shy lately, you sure he solid enough to rock with you like that?"

I had already asked myself that. "Yea I do. He a loyal nigga and he ain't scared to bus his gun Unk. I trust him," I said.

Big Rome nodded his head. "A wise man once told me, 'the only way two people can keep a secret is if one person kills the other'," Big Rome said.

"Naw Unk, I consider him family," I said.

Big Rome just smiled. "Well Nephew if you feel like that, a wise man also told me, 'Blood makes us related, loyalty is what makes us family.' Remember that."

We chopped it up for a few more minutes, then Big Rome had to shoot a move. So, I jumped out the Jag and headed to my new truck. The windows was tinted so you couldn't see inside.

"What the big homie talking bout God?"

"Shit. He fucked up about Lil Mark, we hit hard, they hit harder. We need to knock these niggas off so shit can cool down," I said.

"Yea I know, God and we still gotta find that bitch Peaches."

"Yea I know Shy, so what now? We need to find somebody who know something about them C.B.K. niggas. Them niggas ain't that good," I said angrily.

"I feel you, God. You know what, swing by the hood real quick. I know somebody we can ask. If this nigga don't know then nobody know, you feel me."

We rolled around the hood for a good hour. We couldn't find the person Shy was looking for, so we said fuck it. We went to Shy's house to re-strategize. As we were coming up the block, we noticed a black Cavalier in Shy's driveway.

"Who car is that Shy?"

"Yo guess as good as mine, God."

We pulled up in front of the vacant house next door to Shy's crib then walked up to the car. It was a piece of paper taped to the trunk that said, "open me." Me and Shy looked at each other then we both pulled out our straps simultaneously. We looked around, the block looked dead. I looked down and I noticed the key was already in the trunk's keyhole. I popped the truck looked inside. Damn!

"Guess we can cross looking for Peaches off our list of things to do," Shy said. He was right, Peaches body was folded in the trunk with two holes in her head.

My Spidey senses went off and I scanned the block again. I caught movement to my right and I saw a guy stepping out the doorway of the vacant house. Without thinking I snatched Shy to the ground. **BOC! BOC! BOC! BOC! BOC! BOC! BOC!** We hit the ground hard while the unknown man kept shooting the A.K. I heard a clicking noise and I glanced over the car, the guy was pulling on the slide, trying to release it. It must be jammed! I jumped up and started firing and Shy followed suit. He back peddled and fell through the door of the vacant house. Me and Shy took off running just in time before he came back out firing. **BOC! BOC! BOC! BOC! BOC! BOC!** We jumped a couple fences and hid in somebody garage.

"Fuck, fuck, fuck, I can't believe this shit," Shy screamed.

"Shit! Did you get a good look at that nigga?" I asked.

"Yea God, that's why I'm so pissed."

"Who the fuck was that and why is he tryin to kill us?"

"Man you not gone believe this, but that was a young crazy nigga from Plymouth named Choppa."

"Choppa? Spell it out for me Shy, you not making no sense."

"Look Ali, that was Twerk nephew. He want to kill us for killing his uncle, God."

"Awww Shit!"

Choppa made his way back home, mad as fuck. As long as he had old rusty, that bitch ain't never jammed. He pulled into a driveway and pulled the car all the way to the back. He jumped out the car with the A.K. and jumped the fence into the alley. He walked down the alley and then jumped another fence heading to the next street over. He walked to the back door and opened it, then stepped inside. He did the same routine every time he came home, to prevent people from knowing where his house was. Choppa grabbed some WD40 from the cabinet and popped the clip out of the A.K. He put on some gloves and started oiling up the A.K. He put on some gloves and started oiling up the A.K. so won't jam again. It ain't no secret why his name is Choppa, that's the only gun he ever used. This was the first time he ever missed from that close and it almost cost him his life. He vowed to never let that happen again.

Ali

Me and Shy sat in a dope friend's house named Talkalot on Grand River and Ivanhoe St. Talkalot gives us a tip on where the C.B.K niggas be laying low down the street from his house. Me and Shy had a choppa a piece, with drums on them. After Choppa tried to kill us at Shy's house, we quickly went in and grabbed as much ammo and weapons as we could.

"Look Nephew their go Bay Boy right there pullin up," Talkalot yelled.

I looked out the window and sure as shit Bay Boy was jumping out a black Tahoe truck going to the house we've been watchin for the last hour.

"I told y'all I knew where they be at so give me my shit so I can get high," Talkalot said.

"Chill the fuck out God. I told you imma pay you when we done and we ain't done yet, fucking cluck!" Shy yelled angrily.

I sat at the window trying to come up with the best way to approach the situation then it hit me.

"Aye I got a plan listen up closely, so we can get this done," I said.

As I told both of them the plan I looked in Shy's eyes looking for any fear. I saw none. I see why Mark loved this lil nigga. We went over the plan a couple more times until the sun went down a bit, then we went outside and got in position.

Me and Shy ducked behind a blue Caravan directly behind the truck Bay Boy came out of. Talkalot walked toward the truck and bashed the window out with a crowbar. The alarm went off and he began to hit the car some more. Just like I expected the front door to the house opened and Bay Boy and Tommy came outside. Two for one special I thought.

"Aye, what the fuck is wrong with you bitch. You a dead man!" Bay Boy yelled.

I counted to 10 trying to let them get closer, but something happed that made everything go south. Tommy pulled out two pistols.

"Bro it's a set up don't" …

Before he could finish me and Shy came from behind the van firing.

BOC! BOC! BOC! BOC! BOC! BOC! BOC!

I fired directly at Bay Boy. I watched his back open up as he tried to run back in the house. He fell hard after the second shot hit him and his face hit the bottom stair hard as shit. Tommy, who started shooting at us as soon as we came from behind the van, got lucky. He fired blindly, as he dived through the front window.

The three of us retreated and jumped in a stolen impala we had parked a few houses down and we fled the scene as fast as we could. Shy drove calmly, Talkalot sat in the passenger seat, while I sat directly behind him.

"Y'all muthafuckas crazy! Man they seen my face, they gone kill me man! Y'all got to give me some extra shit!" Talkalot screamed.

Shy looked at me in the rearview mirror and nodded his head. I picked up the choppa I had layin on the seat and I put the barrel to the back of the seat. Shy turned up the radio as loud as it could go.

BOC! BOC! BOC! BOC!

I fired threw the seat knocking everything inside his stomach on the floor.

"Damn God, what the fuck you do that stupid shit for?" Shy asked.

All of a sudden the car started smoking and we pulled over.

"You done shot the damn engine up fool."

"Shit, I didn't feel like choking his ass to death and you got both of the 40s," I said.

Me and Shy got out the car and lifted the head. A bunch of smoke came out. A blue Ram truck pulled up and an older man rolled the window down.

"You boys need some help?" the man asked.

Before I could respond, Shy was on his ass. *Shaking my head. Wrong place wrong time old man.

After we put the old man in with Talkalot we set the car on fire and went about our business. Just a normal day in my life. *Laughing out loud. Murder, money, and mayhem...

CHAPTER 10

Tommy

I sat at the table with two 40 cal.'s in my hand, trying not to cry. First my brother and now Bay Boy, Fuck that the gloves comin off now! I looked at the coke on the table, I grabbed a straw, and snorted hard as I could. The rush felt so good I jumped up and flexed my muscles. I heard a cell phone ring and I looked at Gutta. He talked for maybe 2 minutes then he hung up.

"Load up Tommy, it's time to kill some shit" Gutta said. That's all I needed to hear. We jumped in a stolen mercury and drove to a strip mall on 7 Mile and Telegraph. We rode past the nail salon twice then we parked the car.

"These niggas must think shit sweet, huh?" I said angrily.

Gutta had his calm face on as always. I looked in the mirror and I barely recognized myself. My eyes had bags under them and my dreads hung down over my face nappy as shit. I had two months of new growth. The coke had me anxious to kill something. After about 30 minutes of waiting I was getting irritated.

"What the fuck Gutta! What's taking this hoe

so long to come out?"

"Just chill and be patient nigga. You ain't gone run in there and do it, so just wait until she come out." Gutta said.

This muthafucka know exactly what to say to piss me the fuck off. Before I knew it I was out the door. I walked through the door of the nail salon and a ding went off letting people know I came in. It was so bust everybody was either talking or working. I spotted the woman I was looking for and I approached her.

"Auntie Pam, is that you?" I asked.

She looked at me with a confused look. "I'm sorry, but do I know you?"

I didn't even respond. I pulled out my 40 cal. and shot her right in her forehead. It's time for Ali and Big Rome to feel my wrath!!!

Ali

Words couldn't explain the pain that I felt as me, Big Rome, and Tone sat in Big Rome's new Caddy truck. I swear to God, there's going to be a lot of funerals this week.

"Damn Rome, let me know if you need something! Anything bro just ask," Tone said.

Big Rome just nodded his head. "You know what man…. I need a break from this game. My wife layin in the hospital, in a fuckin coma, barely living, and I just buried my son," Big Rome said. "Tone, imma take you up on yo offer. Imma put all the business in yo hands while I get my head togetha."

"What about Mario?" Tone asked.

"Let me worry about Mario, he'll understand."

"When we gone talk to him?"

"We on are way over there now," Big Rome said.

Tone turned around and looked at me in the back seat.

"You don't think we should drop Ali off first?" Tone asked.

"Naw he good. Right now, y'all two all I got."

Maybe I'm trippin or maybe not, but it seemed like Tone had an attitude. I promised myself I would keep an eye on his ass. We pulled up to a house on Toledo and Junction, in the Southwest area in Detroit. It was mostly Mexicans and shit this way, but one thing everybody had in common was money.

We got out the truck and walked around to the back of the house. First thing I noticed, was damn near everybody in the backyard had on red. A cocky Mexican cat with tattoos everywhere walked up to Big Rome and embraced him.

"I heard about what happened man, how you holdin up?"

"I'm pretty fair for a square Mario."

He looked at me like I was a roach or something. "Yow hi the fuck is this you bring to my house Rome?" Mario asked.

A chubby Mexican with a lot of facial hair walked up with a 50 cal. Dessert Eagle. I pulled out my gun and pointed it at his face. Then everybody in the backyard pulled out guns and pointed them in my direction. Big Rome quickly intervened before it got ugly.

"Whoa whoa, Mario this my nephew Ali the one I was tellin you about."

Mario looked at me and then smiled. "Ooohhh, so you Ali? I hear you're a dangerous man, huh?"

I just looked at him. He smiled again.

"You have five seconds to put your gun down or you die," Mario said.

Now it was my turn to smile. "I don't fear death. I rather die on my feet then live on my knee. So, if you gone shoot five seconds been up," I said.

For a minute, everybody was quiet then Mario started laughing.

"I guess you are as tough as they say. Soto out the gun down I like him."

The chubby Mexican lowered his gun and everyone followed suit. I guess this guy Soto was his muscle. He didn't look dangerous, but I knew firsthand looks can be deceiving.

"My house is your house, make yourself at home," Mario said.

Big Rome and Mario walked off and talked privately, while I watched my surroundings. Tone was drinking a beer looking pissed off. I caught him staring at me, when I looked at him, he turned his head. So, I decided to address it.

"Aye Tone what's up man you got something

on yo chest?" I asked.

"Naw Ali, I just think you moving to wild. Ever since you been home it's been home it's been a black cloud over us man." Tone said angrily.

I was bout to smack the shit out of him, but I thought he was right. Big Rome walked up, before either one of us could say another word.

"Look Tone, I got everything set for you. Be on point and get the money," Big Rome said. "Nephew I'm fin-da drop you off to yo car. I need you to go to the hood and pick a package up from Chuck."

"I got you Unk," I said.

"Cool, when you get it just sit on it for a while. I'm fin-da slide up to the hospital and chill wit my wife. You better make your way up there," Big Rome said.

Even though I didn't want to see my Auntie Pam like that I knew I had to. She would do the same for me.

Ali

I pulled up to the trap house on Monica and honked the horn twice. I honked two more times and still nothing happened. I shook my head and got out the car. I walked up to the door and it was slightly open I pulled my gun and pushed it all the way open. "Aye Chuck, you in here nigga?" I didn't get an answer so I walked to the dining room.

Damn. Chuck was lying on his back, with half of his face off. My Spidey senses kicked in, as I slightly turned, and saw the closet door opening. A dread head with tattoos jumped out with two 40s with extended chips.

BOC! BOC! BOC! BOC! BOC! BOC! BOC!

I spent around to dodge the bullets I tripped over the dead body. That might have saved my life. I started shooting through the wall where I thought he would be as I quickly, ran toward the back door. I got to the door and unlocked it. I looked back and noticed it was Tommy. He started firing again. **BOC! BOC! BOC! BOC!** I felt at least four bullets hit me as I made it through the door and fell down the stairs.

I noticed a black dude with a saw-off shotgun behind a trash can. **BOOM! BOOM!** Me falling down the stairs was unexpected so he missed both shots. I shot him twice in the stomach and he fell down. I reached and grabbed my baby 40 cal. from my ankle holster, just in time to see Tommy trying to come through the door. **BOC! BOC! BOC! BOC!** I fired as I got up and jumped over the fence into the alley. I quickly reminded myself to thank Shy for making me where the ankle holster. Gutta and Tommy both were back on their feet and coming toward me. "You can't hide pussy!" Tommy spazzed.

I reloaded both my guns and got ready to die. "Fuck you pussy y'all barking up the wrong tree," I said. And without warning I jumped up and started firing.

BOC! BOC! BOC! BOC!

They both took cover and fired back, as I made my run for it. I started jumping over fences and running for dear life as bullets whizzed past me. I jumped over another fence and noticed a lady trying to unlock the side door to her house. Without thinking I ran up to her and put the gun to her side.

"Hurry up and open the door before I kill you," I said. She unlocked the door and I quickly pushed her inside and locked the door we walked down the stairs to the basement and I turned the light on, she turned around.

"Trina?"

"Oh my fucking God Ali, what the fuck is wrong with you boy? You almost scared me to death." Trina said with tears in her eyes.

"I'm sorry I didn't realize it was you. Some people were trying to kill me."

"Yea, I heard the gunshots," Trina said.

All of a sudden, I was feeling a little dizzy.

"Oh my God sit down, are you okay?"

"I think I got shot a couple times help me take off my shirt," I said.

Trina helped me take my shirt off and I looked at the bulletproof vest I had on. I unfastened it, took it off, and looked at my body. "No bullets went through. It feels like I broke my fuckin ribs tho," I said.

Trina started touching the bruises on my chest and back, I inhaled the scent of her lotion. Vanilla. Last time I saw her was at Marks funeral and she still as beautiful as she was then. I looked over her body and face; she was sexy as fuck with that red hair. Her ass was so fat; my dick got hard just being close to her. She looked me in my eye and I could tell she was feeling the same thing as me. I leaned in and kissed her and her lips were soft and tasted like cherry. She pulled away from me and shook her head.

"What's the matter Trina?"

"I can't do this with you Ali. The life you live is just too dangerous for me."

I looked her dead in her eyes "Do you trust me?" I asked. She held my stare and nodded her head. I pulled out both of my guns. "I would never let anything happen to you."

She took a deep breath and leaned in for another kiss. First, I took it slow because I thought that's what she wanted, but she flipped the script on me. "Hurry up and give me that dick." So, I went into full savage mode. I took all her clothes off and just stared at her. "What's the matter Ali, you scared?"

I stripped asshole naked!!! I got on the couch and slid between her legs. Her pussy was so tight, I had to ease my way in.

"Damn girl! How long it's been since you fucked?"

"6 months daddy," Trina replied.

Once I got in I got my rhythm on point, her legs started shaking as she came all over my dick. "Damn that was easy," I teased.

"Shut the fuck up nigga and fuck me." Okay, that's enough with being Mr. Nice Guy. I grabbed her ankles and pushed them all the way back to her ears. "No daddy it hurt," Trina cried. It didn't matter I'm fin-da kill this pussy.

I started beating that shit up and Trina was screaming like somebody was killing her. I guess I was. I put her legs down and made her assume the position. Face down, ass up, and arch yo back. I had her pussy so wet her juices was running down my nuts to the floor. I been so occupied with murder, this just what I needed to relax me. I felt myself about to come, so I drilled harder. My whole body ached from the gun shots the vest took. As I busted a fat nut inside of Trina, my mind was already back on murder.

I laid back on the couch thinking about my next move and Trina kissed my face. "What you thinking about?" Trina asked.

"I was thinking you're just what I needed," I responded.

"You probably tell all the hoes that."

"Naw mama, when I say something, I mean it."

We chilled for a minute then she got personal.

"Why don't you never talk about your mother or father?" Trina asked.

That question kind of threw me off. I looked in her eyes and I told myself that if I make it to see 22, I was gone marry her. "Honestly, I never knew my Pops. My mom was a crack fiend who sold her pussy to get high. When I was 10, she overdosed on heroin. My Auntie Pam took me in and took care of me. She's the only mother I got." I didn't even realize that I was crying. I promised myself I was gone kill Tommy,

Gutta, Choppa, and anybody else who I feel need to go.

"It's okay Ali. Sorry I bring it up," Trina said.

"It's okay Lil mama I needed to get it out."

"Bae yo phone keep vibrating," Trina said.

I grabbed it and realized it was Shy. "What's up fool?"

"Shit God, just checkin on you."

"Aye, them C.B.K. niggas just tried to slump me, if I ain't have the vest I would-a been done," I said angrily.

"What! Where you at nigga?" Shy asked.

"I'll get at you later Shy. Lay low until I call you bro."

"Alright God I got you," Shy said.

I hung up and dove back in some pussy.

Shy

After I got off the phone with Ali, I was beyond pissed. Even though I just met him he like a big brother to me. I got a small apartment on 6 mile and evergreen to lay back in. Shit been so crazy I ain't had no chill time, period. Fuck it, I got dressed, grabbed about 15 bands out of one of my shoe boxes, and jumped in my low-key Commander truck.

I ended up at *Hot Tamales* on 8 Mile. I walked in with a pink dolphin outfit on. I had a *Rolex* on fully blown and some all-white Buffs or *Cartier* glasses for y'all who don't know. The place was packed cause it was Saturday, but it seem like wasn't no rich nigga's in the buildin, so I knew I was about to go crazy. My man Joker the bouncer at the door, so you know I had my ratchet with me.

I peeped a bad brown skin chic, thick as fuck, watchin me. I reached in my jacket pocket and pulled out a half ounce of some Cookie. Sat it on the table and pulled out some Backwoods. She winked her eye, and I waved her over to my table.

"Hey daddy, I see you smoking good can I hit that?" she asked.

"That's funny I was thinkin the same shit about hittin that." I said with a smirk.

"I hear that slick shit boy," she said.

I pulled out a big roll of money and her eyes lit up. "Go get me 5,000 in singles and bring me a fifth of Remy 1738," I said.

She took the money and walked away giving me a good view of that ass. I started rolling up Backwoods as I watched my surroundings. After about 15 minutes, baby girl came back with a garbage bag with my money in it and my fifth of Remy. I looked in the bag and I saw a bunch of hundred-dollar rolls unwrapped them, then made it rain on lil mama.

"Okay I see you, big money," she said.

"Yea, you know how Fenkell niggas get down." I boasted.

"Okay, Fenkell niggas in the house tonight."

I looked around the club again. "Ain't none of these bum ass niggas from my way." I said cocky with it.

She pointed to the corner by the bar where a bunch of lames was standing at.

"See look at ole boy sittin down with the dreads he reppin 4-1 all day," she said.

I took off my glasses and looked closer and my eyes popped out of my socket. I can't believe this shit. Tommy was sittin at the bar talkin to strippers. It's so many niggas flocking the bar I never noticed him. I'm glad I saw him first because if the shoe was on the other foot I would be dead.

"You okay daddy? You look pissed," the stripper asked.

"Naw I'm cool sexy. Go grab me another drink," I said handing her some more money. Without even thinking I pulled out my gun and placed it on my lap.

She looked at the gun, then me, then at Tommy. "Hold up!" she told me. "If you fin-da do some dumb shit you might wanna know it's cameras everywhere." I looked in her eyes and I saw a ride or die bitch I decided to test her gangsta.

"What's your name sexy?"

"Brandy, why?"

"My name Shy lil mama."

"Okay, and what do that supposed to mean?" Brandy asked with a sassy tone that turned me on.

"You know where the tape at to the camera feed?"

"Yea."

I reached in my pocket and gave her my car keys and the bag of money. "I want you to get all the tapes and take it to my truck. It's a Black Commander truck you can't miss it. Pull the car up to the door and open the driver door. Keep the car running and wait for me." She looked like she wanted to say something, but she chose not to and walked off.

I waited for 20 minutes, watching Tommy drink liquor like water. Once I was sure Brandy was in place, I knew it was time to make my move. I looked around the room again the I got up and walked toward Tommy. I bumped my way through the crowd and made my way to him. His killer instincts must have kicked in because he jerked his head in my direction and tried to reach for his gun.

BOC! BOC! BOC! He was too slow, I shot him three times in the stomach, but the damn bartender came up with the shotgun.

BOOM! Lucky for me he hit a stripper trying to run pass me.

BOC! BOC! BOC! BOC! I fired a couple shots at the bartender, while I made my way to the exit.

When I got outside, Brandy was right where she was supposed to be. I jumped in the truck and sped off.

Brandy looked at me and licked her lips "you crazy as fuck Shy."

Instead of responding I just pulled out my dick. Baby girl sucked the soul out of me all the way back to my apartment. Yea, I like her.

Big Rome

I sat in the hospital watching over my wife in tears. Damn I feel like all of this is my fault. The doctors come in every hour to check her status, but nothing changes. I said a silent prayer up to God and asked him to spare my wife. My cell phone started ringing I looked at the screen and it said Ali.

"What up, Nephew?"

"Shit Unk, where you at?"

"At the hospital, you know that."

"You alone?"

"Yea, why?"

"I'll be there in 20 minutes," Ali said.

Now I was kind of confused. Why did Ali want to know if I was alone or not? As much as I loved Ali, I'm starting to realize he's an accident waiting to happen. I was sitting down wondering should I quit the game before I lose my life, when I heard the door open.

"How's she doin Unk?"

"She still on the breathing machine, but there's lots of activity in her brain."

I looked at Ali and Shy and I had to smile inwardly. These guys are the true meaning of 'you are who you hang around.'

"Aye Shy, you mind standing outside while I talk to Ali?" Shy looked at Ali and Ali nodded his head, then Shy walked out and closed the door behind him. "What's on yo mind nephew?" I asked.

For a minute, he just stood there looking at his Auntie Pam. Then he shook his head and addressed me.

"Look Unk, I know you don't want to hear this right now, but it needs to be said... I'm almost 100% sure that yo home boy Tone, been behind Marks death and my Auntie hanging on to her life."

I looked at Ali like he was the stupidest man on earth. "Come on now Ali. I know you don't really know Tone like that, but that's my mans from the sandbox," I argued.

"Unk, I wouldn't give a fuck if y'all came out the same pussy!!! He foul, think about it. You sent Mark to hit a run that Tone couldn't make it to. Then when y'all sent me to get Pooh, he was already dead. On top of that you send me to pick up a package and I almost get killed. Now who else knew I was on my way besides him?"

I put my head down because Ali was starting to make sense. I knew that if I agreed with Ali, Tone was good as dead. But, I wanted to talk to him first, ask why?

"Tone not cut like that Nephew." If looks could kill, the way Ali looked at me I would've been dead.

"You know what man, you ain't shit but a pussy hiding behind money!' Ali said. I looked Ali right in the eyes to let him know I wasn't scared. "Yea I said it. Yo son dead, yo wife in a coma, and you still on yo head playin Chess. Instead of being on the front like with me." Ali looked at me waiting for a respond, but I didn't have one. "I tell you what Mr. Big Shot, if my Auntie die, you might as well dig you a grave right next to her. In my eyes, if you ain't part of the solution on that thinking man." With that Ali turned around and left.

HOUSE OF PAIN

Chapter 11

Tone

I sat on the couch at one of my trap houses, letting dope fiend Tamika suck my dick. I paid her rent and kept the monkey off her back and in exchange she let me cook and bag up work, when I need to. I grabbed the plate off the table next to me and I took another sniff of the heroin on it. Man, Heaven on earth. I knew my habit was getting out of hand but fuck it! I am the dope man!

That's the real reason I started lying to Big Rome about the robberies. Wasn't nobody stupid enough to run off with my work, not with the team of killas I got. Well, had. It's a shame too because I had a lot more work for them. Deep down I was hurt because I really didn't want Mark to die. I wanted Rome dead! We grew up togetha our whole life, but I was secretly envious of Rome. He always had the prettiest girls, the best clothes, and everybody liked him. Even when he put me down and gave me half the empire, everybody still called me Big Rome's homeboy.

After Mark died things really got out of control. Somehow, this muthafucka Ali finds out

ANDRE CALVIN LEE JR

about Juice, I don't know how but he did. Then he kills him and that makes Tommy go crazy. It was already a close call getting Pooh out the way, but now Tommy's out of control. This crazy muthafucka kills Keisha and Baby Mark. Now I'm trying to cover my tracks, but I keep falling short. Big Rome tells me he's taking Pam to get her nails done. Usually he waits outside for he, but not that day. Then Tommy fuckin shoots Pam! What the fuck? On top of that, I delivered Ali to them on a silver platter and they missed. Now, Tommy laid up in a hospital somewhere and Gutta's nowhere to be found.

I took another sniff of the heroin as I felt myself about to come. I grabbed Tamika by the back of her head and made her swallow everything. I sat back with my head spinning and a thousand thoughts ran through my head. I heard my phone start to ring and I looked at the screen Gutta. Okay, back in action.

Ali

Me and Shy sat in a rental I had Trina get for me. We were on Nevada St. between John R. and Charleston. We've been sitting out here for an hour and a half waiting for Tone to come out.

"You sure he in here Shy?" I asked.

"Yea God, Tamika know not to like to me. Plus, she owes me. It's either this or I collect in blood," Shy said.

I looked at the tattoos on his face, No Luv No

Fear, he defiantly lives up to that. I scanned the block again making sure that we weren't getting set up.

"Look, somebody coming out God."

I looked up and sure as shit I saw Tone coming out jumping into an old Ford Taurus. I have to admit; Tone knew how to stay under the radar. He never dressed flashy or anything of the sort.

I pulled out behind him and made sure I stayed back enough not to be noticed. He made a right on John R. and then once he got to 6 Mile he made another right. He kept straight down 6 Mile, until he crossed Livernois. He drove a couple of blocks down, then made a right on San Juan. It was a liquor store on the corner of San Juan and 6 Mile. When I turned the corner, I noticed that Tone stopped in the middle of the block. I pulled on the side of the store and stopped just in case he looked back my car won't look out of place.

"What you think he doin Shy?"

"I don't know God," Shy responded. He grabbed a blunt from behind his ear and fired it up. "Aye, you know what I was thinkin God? We should go in on like a double date, that way you can meet my new lady. Shit, I already know Trina." I looked at Shy and I bust out laughing. "Yo what the fuck you laughin at, I'm serious."

"My bad Shy, I ain't never heard you on no soft shit that's all." I said still laughing.

"Come on God, you know my get down. Ain't no shit soft about me. Sometimes a nigga just need a break, you feel me."

I didn't have to respond. All I been seeing is death since I was released from prison, so I knew exactly what he meant.

"Look God, somebody pullin up on Tone. He must be meeting somebody," Shy said.

I saw a black Mustang pulling up and parked right behind Tone. A black dude with a bald head jumped out with a A.K. with a drum on it in his hands. The bald man walked to the passenger side of Tones car and stuck the A.K. through the window. I thought he was about to kill Tone, but the bald man adjusted the A.K. so the handle was sticking out the window. Smart! Any real killa know being trapped in a car during a gun fight is deadly. Instead, he just stood outside the car with his hand on the handle of the A.K. watching his surroundings in case shit jumped off.

"Aye Shy, am I trippin or I that Gutta?"

Shy leaned all the way up. "Damn God, you was right. Slide down on them. Imma jump out and give both they ass the business." Shy said geeked up.

"Naw Shy, I know you saw that drum on that yop he had? All we got is two glocks on us. We gotta let'em slide this time," I said full of disappointment.

Shy nodded his head because he knew I was right. "So, what now? We keep following Tone?" Shy asked.

"Naw, I seen enough." With that, I pulled off and rode pass two people I plan on killing real soon.

I pulled up to Mark's house so I could give Trina the rental and I jumped back in my truck. I told her to go home and get dressed because we were going out tonight. Me and Shy got in my truck and my cell phone went off. I look at the screen and saw it was Big Rome.

"What up! You ready to ride?" I asked angrily.

"Hey Ali, what you doin boy?"

As soon as I heard that voice my whole day got brighter. "Auntie Pam, I knew you was gone pull through, we got the same blood line."

"Yea, the good Lord blessed me baby."

"When can you go home?"

"The doctors want me to stay for a month and go to therapy. But, you know Rome got the best doctors in Michigan on call ready to service me at home. So imma stay two more days, then I'm going home."

"That's what's up Auntie, I love you."

"I love you too, baby."

Choppa

I pulled up to a house on Stoepel and Norfolk right off 8 Mile and Livernois. I looked in the rearview mirror at my wild afro and shook my head. I needed my hair done bad, that's why I'm where I am now. I pulled in the driveway and honked my horn twice once I saw the side door open. I grabbed my A.K. off the passenger seat and jumped out the car.

"Damn Choppa, to paranoid ass always got that A.K. wit you boy!"

I just laughed at her as I walked through the door.

"Hi, to you too Mr. Attitude," she said.

"Come on now Brandy, you know I love you fool. Come on and braid my hair, so I can slide." I said with my trademark smile on my face.

"Okay Daddy, you got it."

I know I had Brandy right where I wanted her, which was wrapped around my finger. She grabbed the supplies she needed to braid my hair. I sat on the floor between her legs, while brandy began to braid. While Brandy braided my hair, I rolled a blunt. Once it was rolled and fired up, I got down to business.

"So... I heard it was a shooting at yo job the other day?" I asked nonchalantly.

"Yea Daddy, that dumb ass young nigga almost killed a nigga on camera. But, I knew you wanted him personally so I helped him get away," Brandy said.

I just nodded my head. I been fuckin Brandy since she was 16. I taught her everything she know. I was going to have her set up Ali and Shy. It was just dumb luck Shy went to Hot Tamales that night.

"Do he trust you," I asked.

"A little bit."

"That's not enough Brandy, what the fuck!" I said angrily.

"Please don't get mad at me I'm doing everything you want me to do Chris," she called me by my real name because she knew she would calm me down. She knew how to get to me, also.

"I'm sorry Love, when is the next time you get to see Shy?" I asked.

"Tonight around 10:00," Brandy said.

"Okay, finish braiding me up so I can leave. You remember what to do right?"

"Yes, you told me a million times daddy."

A couple hours went past, and it was getting close to 10:00. I grabbed my A.K. off the floor and headed toward the door. Before I stepped completely out I scanned my surroundings, looking for any sign of trouble. Once I was certain it was clear, I jumped in my truck and backed out the driveway. I parked a couple houses down from Brandy's house, then hit my lights and waited for Shy to pull up.

After I smoked my second blunt, I noticed an all-black Camaro pulling on Brandy's driveway. Just like I did, he honked the horn twice and Brandy came out. I debated on doing it now, but I didn't want to make Bandy's house a crime scene. So, I followed them. I stayed two cars behind while Shy drove up Livernois. He made a right on 7 Mile, so I followed suite. Once we got to Wyoming it was a red light.

Out of nowhere Shy ran through the red light, almost crashing into cars coming in the opposite direction. At this point I realized he knew I was following him, so I didn't go after him. I know I can count on Brandy to tell me where I need to be. And just like that to my phone. *We going to club encore on 7 Mile and Greenfield.* So, I hit the gas and tried to get there first.

When I pulled in the gas station across the street, I scanned the cars looking for Shy. **BEEP!** Another text. *We stopped for some weed.* Cool! I pulled up in front of the club then paid valet to park in the small parking lot. I sat for ten minutes, then I saw the Camaro pull in. I knew this pussy would park his car back here. I jumped out the truck and ran behind another truck to hide myself, but still in a position to strike. I checked my A.K., then I double checked it. I pulled the mask over my face and got ready for action. That's when shit started to go south. Once the driver door opened the I expected to see Shy but no, it was Brandy. Brandy leaned down and hit the lever to push the driver seat up then Shy came out the backseat. Once he got out he instantly grabbed Brandy and pulled her close to him. The way Shy scanned the parking lot, I knew that he knew that I was out there. So, fuck it I stepped out.

"I finally caught up with you, huh Shy?"

Shy placed a 45. to Brandy's head and smiled. "If that cheap ass choppa jam again you ain't gone be so lucky," Shy said.

"What my uncle do so bad that he had to pay the price of his life?" I asked.

I was starting to get pissed off. I heard commotion to my right, and I turned to see what it was. Big Mistake. **BOC! BOC! BOC!** Shy started shooting, while moving backwards holding Brandy like a shield. A 45-slug hit my chest and I almost fell on my face. At that point I said fuck Brandy. **BOC! BOC! BOC!** I tried to shoot the door down! As if shit wasn't bad enough, I turn around and see a police car pulling up fast. Before they had a chance to tell me to drop my gun, I Swiss Cheesed they ass. **BOC! BOC! BOC! BOC!** I heard the yop click and I knew it was empty. I heard police sirens in the distance and the first thing that came to my mind was the two choppa clips in the back of my car and the Ruger in the stash. I hurried up and ran toward my car and I got to the truck just in time before the police pulled up three cars deep. I quickly grabbed the choppa clips and Ruger and I jumped out the car and hid behind.

"This is the Detroit Police Tactical Team. Please drop your weapon and come out peacefully," one officer said.

I started to feel dizzy, and I remembered I was shot. My shirt was soaked; I was losing a lot of blood fast. I thought about giving up, but when I peeped over the truck I noticed the first police car that pulled up had no survivors. Fuck that! I took a couple deep breaths. **BOC! BOC! BOC!** The police scattered like I knew they would, which gave me a chance to run toward the back of the parking lot. I jumped on a car and jumped over the fence; I landed in the alley. I jumped another fence into somebody's backyard and almost got chewed up by a Pitbull. **BOC! BOC!** No more Puppy Chow for yo ass. Once I got to the front yard, police cars were just bending the corner. **BOC! BOC! BOC! CLICK! CLICK! CLICK!** I tried to grab my other clip, but an officer shot me in the stomach twice. I laid there with my eyes closed while two officers approached me to make sure I'm dead. When they were close enough, I fired the Ruger. **BOC! BOC! BOC!** One of the officers dropped, but the other officer shot me about six more times. About 50 officers grabbed me up placed my heads behind my back then kicked me back to the ground.

"Jesus Chuck, this guy is going to die if we don't get him to a hospital."

The officer named Chuck stared at me for a while, then he addressed his partner.

"Ten" Officer Chuck said.

His partner was just as confused as me. "Ten what?"

"That's how many officers he killed tonight buddy, Ten."

I saw both officers turn around and leave me there. I saw all the blood leaving my body and then, I saw nothing. Before my body completely shut down, I smiled knowing that I took ten of them dick suckers with me.

Tone

I pulled up to a mini mansion in the Sherwood Forest community. I got out the car, walked up to the house, and rung the bell. A short chubby Mexican, who I remember Mario calling Sato, opened the door. He checked me then led me to the basement, where the meeting was held. I was kind of taken back when I got downstairs and saw nothing, but Mario with his shirt playing with an all-white Pitbull with a black patch on his right eye.

"What's going on Mario? It looks like I'm a little early," I said with a nervous laugh.

"No Tone, you're right on time. Take a seat please," Mario said. I walked over to the round table Mario had built in the floor of the basement and took a seat. After a minute, he came to the table and sat down. For a minute, he just looked at me. I had a real bad feeling. "So... what's on your mind Tone?" Mario asked in a friendly tone.

"Ut, okay, uh I need... I mean, me and Rome need more work this month," I said.

Mario raised his eyebrow, like The Rock used to do. "Why do you guys need more work? Last time I checked you went from coppin 30 to 15 a piece. Then y'all dropped to 25."

"Listen I'm not gone lie to you, I love Rome, but he been slippin. I had a talk with him a couple weeks ago about spending too much," I lied.

"So Big Rome was the one slacken?"

"Yea, plus it's too much goin on around him now, with the murders and police. That's why he passed the dealings on to me."

Mario closed his eyes, like he was in deep thought. Then his eyes popped open. "How much we talkin?" Mario asked.

When he said that I knew I had to use my word play to make it work.

"I need a 100!"

"Whoa, whoa! 100? That's a big leap Tone, I don't know about that."

Shit okay think Tone, think! BINGO! It came to

me what Mario liked, quick money.

"Listen Mario I know you skeptical but, just listen. I already got major buyers in Philly and Pittsburgh and I'm taxin them 120,000 a brick. It's like heroin heaven down there." I could see the wheels on Mario's head spinning.

"How fast is the come back?"

"Well with the clientele I already got, plus the new ones in Pennsylvania and a possible line in Florida, imma have half of the money in 10 days," I said confidently.

"Yea right."

"I swear, you give me 100 keys of heroin for 60,000 a pop. I will gladly bring you 6 million dollars in less than a month."

"Okay, okay, imma give you a chance. But, remember if something go wrong it's on you and Rome."

"Okay, I understand."

"I'll call you in an hour and tell you where to go and get a moving truck. Once you're in the truck they're your responsibility," Mario said.

I got up and left feeling like the king. Little do Mario know, this is the last time he'll ever see me.

Tommy

I'm laid up in this fucking hospital, feeling like a bitch. I took a couple to the stomach and now, I got to wear this shit bag for 6 months to a year! What the fuck! Every time I look at this shit bag I think of Shy. I put that on my brother's life, I'm killin him, Ali, and everybody them niggas love. My stomach growled again, and I thought about the nurse I sent to get my food damn near 20 minutes ago. Fuck it! I climbed out the bed, which was harder than I expected but I did it. I opened the door and I almost jumped for Joy. The nigga Big Rome pushing his wife up the hallway in a wheelchair. I thought I killed that bitch, I guess not huh? I closed the door a little bit and eased dropped on their conversation.

"I can't wait to go home today bae."

"I know love, we got to wait for the paperwork though to see what kind of meds you need," Big Rome said.

Fuck that I be damned if they make it out this hospital. I walked back to the bed and the nurse walked in with my food on a try.

"Here's your food sir," the nurse said.

"Fuck that food, where my clothes?"

"Sir, I have to advise you that you can mess"-

"Bitch shut the fuck up and give me my shit."

With that she went and got my clothes with the quickness. I put them on, blood stains and all, and got the fuck up out of there. I pulled my phone out my bag they had it in and called bro.

"Damn Bitch, I been waitin on yo call!"

"Fuck that, where you at Gutta?"

"Close by you know that."

"Get here fast and bring some guns!"

I made it to the front door without Big Rome spotting me. I got a couple of crazy looks from people, but fuck'em. When I got outside, I had to bum a cigarette from somebody, while I waited for Gutta. He pulled up in a 2015 Mustang.

"What up lil bro," Gutta said as I jumped in the car.

"You bring the guns?"

"You know that."

While we parked in a 15-minute parking space, I told Gutta what was what, while I loaded my 40. We ended up waiting three more hours before Big Rome came out.

"Look here they come," I said to Gutta.

"Bro fuck that 40 take this Mac," Gutta said.

I grabbed the Mac, covered it up with my shirt and jogged toward Big Rome. About time he noticed me it was too late. **BOC! BOC! BOC! BOC! BOC! BOC!** I shot the bitch in the wheelchair so many times, the whole wheelchair flipped. Big Rome pussy ass ran back in the hospital, but I still shot him twice in the back. I ran to the whip and Gutta fishtailed out the hospital parking lot. I was so hype I was jumping up and down in my seat.

"Yea, if that hoe survive that, I'm taking her ass to the casino," I laughed.

I looked at Gutta and his face was tore up. "What's the matter Bro?" I asked.

"What the fuck is that smell Tommy?"

I lift my shirt up I saw shit everywhere.

"Aww Shit."

Ali

Damn! That's the only thing that I can think of as I watched Trina suck the shit out of my dick. I never thought that I would ever feel the way that I feel now. Is this love? Hell Naw, not me! So why have I been at Trina's house for a whole week without leaving. I even turned my phone off. I know Shy ass probably going crazy looking for me. Damn! I came hard as fuck and Trina swallowed every drop.

"You like that baby?"

"You know that."

"Nigga you ain't got to always be tough, at least not with me. So, did you like it?"

"I ain't got to explain what's already understood," I said.

She got the point and left it alone. Trina laid on top of me and it felt like, I could've laid here forever. "What's wrong, Ali?"

"Nothing."

"You don't have to lie to me," Trina said.

"I was just thinking about my Auntie that's all. I haven't been to see her since she woke up," I said.

"Call her, we can go see her together." I looked in Trina's eyes and all I saw was loyalty. I grabbed my phone and turned it on and immediately it started ringing. It was Shy!

"What's good fool?"

"What the fuck you mean what's good? Where you been fool? Niggas tryna kill me God. The bitch Brandy set me up!"

I instantly jumped up. "What, slow down Shy

where you at?"

"I'm at The House of Pain bro, get here!" Shy hung up before I could respond.

"I got to go Trina, Shy's in some type of trouble. I'll call you later."

"Okay, be safe Ali."

"You know that." I quickly got dressed, grabbed my 45 from under the bed and I left.

I wonder what the fuck Shy is doing as The House of Pain. Shy once told me about a house that he used to take people to and torture. I thought it was a joke, until he took me there. The house smelled like death, from all the blood and body fluids. My phone rang again, this time it was Big Rome. I sent his ass to voicemail; I'll holla at him later. I pulled up to The House of Pain, Shy was in the doorway. I parked my truck and walked through the basement. Shy filled me in on how Brandy and Choppa tried to put the play down on him. Once we got to the basement, I looked at Brandy with no sympathy, period. She was tied up on the floor layin in her own vomit and blood.

"Damn Brandy, you ain't lookin to good," I said with a smirk. "What you gone do with her Shy?"

Shy looked at me, then at Brandy. He smiled a demonic smile and I swear I thought I saw the devil. Shy ran upstairs and came back down quickly with a gas can and a bunch of water. Shy walked over to Brandy as I watched, with a confused face, Shy snatch the tape off Brandy's mouth.

"Let's play a little game brandy," Shy said.

"Shy I'm so sorry he made me do it, he said he was gone kill me!" Brandy cried.

"Oh okay, so you traded my life instead of yours?" Brandy didn't say anything then. "It's okay, you don't have to answer me. Right now, I'm going to give you a chance to repent," Shy said.

Big Rome kept blowing up my phone. I ain't trying to hear no lectures right now. So, I kept sending him to voicemail.

"Listen up Brandy, I'm going to ask you a question and your answer will determine whether you go to Hell or Heaven." Shy said. "If I decide you go to Heaven, I'm going to drown you in this bucket of water. If you go to hell…"

Shy picked up the gas can and set it back down. Brandy broke down crying because she knew she was dead regardless.

"Okay, so if I let you live would you got to the police?" Shy asked Brandy.

Brandy was crying so hard, she had snot coming out her nose. Shy punched her in the face with all his might. Shy then poured the gas all over her body, lit a piece of paper on fire, and threw it on Brandy. Let me tell you. I'm a real nigga to the death of me, but the smell of burnt skin almost made me lose my lunch. Me and Shy watched her burn until he poured the water on her. The fire didn't go out, so he used a fire extinguisher. The basement was so smoky, me and Shy had to go outside. We jumped in my truck, and we bounced, before somebody saw the smoke and called the police.

"Aye God, you a strong nigga. I thought you would be going crazy about Pam, I'm kinda shocked." Shy said.

"What the fuck you talkin bout Shy?"

Shy looked at me with wide eyes and shook his head. "Pull over God."

Ali

Me and Shy rode in silence on our way to our destination. I felt like whatever soul, mercy, or love that I had left in my body. I looked over at Shy. The only family I got left, the only person I trust, a little bit! We pulled up to a big brick house in Westland. Big Rome came outside and looked 20 years older. Shy opened the door and jumped out.

"Sit in the front O.G. I know you got a lot to talk about," Shy said.

Big Rome just nodded his head as he climbed in my truck. Shy got in the back.

"Nephew man, where you been man? I been callin you and shit man, shit crazy." Big Rome said.

I never even looked his way, but I heard him crying. "What happened Rome?" I asked, still not looking directly at him.

"That young nigga with the dreads caught me slippin pushing yo Auntie out the hospital. I ain't have a gun I couldn't do shit. I got shot a couple times, too." Big Rome said, like that made the situation better.

I lost all respect I ever had for Big Rome.

"So how is you alive and my Auntie not? Wasn't it in yo wedding vowels to protect yo wife till death do y'all part?" I said getting angry.

"Nephew, I can't fight a gun."

"Y'all should've died together." I finally looked at him. "When's the funeral Rome?" I asked.

"Saturday. I got everything set up and paid for already," Big Rome said.

"Let me tell you a story Rome," I said. "A scorpion was walking through the woods, and he ended up at a pond that he couldn't cross. Why? Cause scorpions can't swim. So, a frog comes be and the scorpion says, 'hey frog, I need a ride across the pond.' The frog says no! You're a scorpion if I give you a ride you'll sting me. Scorpion says, 'I promise I won't sting you. I'm just looking for a ride.' So, against the frog's better judgment, he gives the scorpion a ride. They made it all the way to the other side and the frog says we're here. Scorpion says thanks then he stings the frog. Frog says, 'why'd you sting me.' Scorpion says, 'because I'm a scorpion, I sting people.' Moral of the story, you can't help what you are. Me; imma killa, Shy; he's a killa, You; you a Pussy. It's on yo nature to be a pussy because that's what you are." I said nodding my head. I put my hand out for a handshake. "See you at the funeral," I said. Big Rome grabbed my hand and shook it. **BOC! BOC!** Brains everywhere.

"What the fuck Shy? I said kill him when he got out dumb ass!"

"Push him outside then, God."

116

I pushed Big Rome outside and we pulled off.

"I swear to God Shy, you payin for my car to get cleaned," I said seriously.

"Yea whatever muthafucka, let's go holla at Cook, so we can get some more guns," Shy said.

I smiled and shook my head. I wonder, is the city of Detroit ready for what the fuck I'm about to do? Me and Shy about to kill any and everybody that I feel roll with Tommy, Gutta, Tone, and whoever else. The gloves off now.

SHOWTIME!

Chapter 12

Ali

After me and Shy hollered at Cook, I felt a lot better about what I was about to do. We got choppas, A.R.'s, Mini 114's, Mac 90's, Tech 9's, 40's, Desert Eagles, and a couple of bulletproof vests. I looked at Shy loading up a couple of the guns we had and made me think of Mark. This whole thing started because of Mark, and now look; this shit spiraled out of control. I wondered, was Mark upset with me about killing Big Rome? Or what about Keisha, also Lil Mark and Auntie Pam?

Shy's cell phone rung and he answered it and began talking. I was lost in my own thoughts thinking about Mark when Shy hung up the phone happy as shit.

"Aye God, I got some good news!"

"You found Tommy?" I asked.

"Naw, not that good. But I did find Tones sneaky ass," Shy said.

I nodded my head approvingly because I should've been cashed his ticket in. "Let's go get him," I said to Shy. And with that, we grabbed our straps and got ready to take care of business.

Me and Shy pulled up to an apartment complex on Village Rd. right off 15 Mile and Gratiot. We pulled up in front of the complex and just sat there surveying the surroundings making sure it wasn't a set up.

"Run it down to me again, Shy."

"Look God, this lil hoe named Tanika I used to rob niggas with back in the day, called me and said, Tone been over here for 3 days getting high and fuckin her." Shy said.

"So, why she just callin you today then?" I asked.

"Because at first she was just fuckin with the nigga to pay her rent, but then she overheard him on the phone; tellin somebody to hurry up and kill Ali and Shy."

I shook my head because pussy always a weak nigga downfall. I swear, I ain't never trust a bitch, since Eve ate that forbidden fruit.

"Have you ever slumped a nigga around her?" I asked Shy.

"Hell Naw, God. It's sad to say that bitch was dead the moment she involved herself in this shit," Shy said like he was casually talking about a game.

I looked at Shy long and hard. I once heard somebody say that it's impossible for two real niggas to hang around each other. The old saying goes, if two real niggas hang together one of them is actually, fake or pretending in so many words. I know I'm far from fake and if Shy was fake or pretending, he was doing a damn good job at it. Shy looked at me like he could read my mind.

"It's death before dishonor with me God, from the cradle to the grave." Shy said.

Before I could respond the front door to the apartment opened and a thick ass dark skin beauty came down toward my truck. She waved her hand for us to come on, so we jumped out the car and followed her.

"Where the fuck Tone at Tanika?" Shy asked exactly what I was thinking.

She just smiled at us. "You'll see boy," she said.

I stopped at the same time as Shy.

"Naw fuck that lil mama, answer the question." I said in a serious tone.

"Damn Shy, tell ya mans to relax. If I was tryna set y'all up why would I do it at my house." She said with a lot of attitude.

Me and Shy looked at each other and said fuck it. We followed her in the house to the back bedroom. We both had our guns drew as we entered the room, but it was no need. Tone was laying on the bed nodding in and out like a dope fiend slobbering on his self. I looked at the dresser and it was a kilo of heroin opened, with lines on a small mirror. Shy bust out laughing.

"Damn God, ya mans got a monkey on his back, huh?" Shy said.

I, on the other hand, didn't find shit funny. It all started to make sense to me. This nigga tried to kill Big Rome because he couldn't afford his drug habit and he mistakenly, killed Mark. I lost rest of the little family that I had because this fat bitch wanted to get high.

"Go get some ice lil mama," I said. Tanika ran to the kitchen and came back with two ice trays. "Put some ice under his nuts," I said.

"He ain't overdosed," Shy pointed out.

"I know, it's still gone wake him up."

Tanika did as she was told, and Tone fat ass jumped up quick as shit. He took one look at me and Shy and I'm pretty sure he shit his pants.

"What's up Nephew? What you doin?" Tone said trying to cover up his dick.

"I ain't yo fuckin Nephew, nigga. You got a lot of explaining to do Tone and I'm not in the mood for bullshit," I said.

"What you talkin about Ali?" Tone asked.

I didn't even respond. I pointed my gun at Tanika and blew half her fuckin face off. **BOC!** She hit the ground with a thud, then I shot her two more times in the chest. **BOC! BOC!**

"You still want to keep playin crazy Tone?" I asked in heated voice.

"Okay, okay, okay, what you want to know?" Tone asked.

"Where Tommy and Gutta hiding?" I asked him.

Tone took too long to answer, so I shot him in his dick. **BOC!**

"Ahhhh! Shit okay man, I'll tell you Ali please don't shoot me again." And the next 20 minutes, that's what he did.

Tone told me everything we needed to know. After he was done talking, he looked up at me with puppy dog eyes, "Please don't kill me Ali, I swear to God I'll give you whatever you want. Just don't kill me please."

"Shut the fuck up!" I said. I couldn't believe after everything this pussy caused; he got the nerve to ask for mercy. "Okay Tone, I got you," I said nodding my head.

I heard the front door close; I turned around and saw Shy coming back in. I sent Shy to the drug store while Tone was spilling his guts.

"You got what I need Shy?"

"Yes, God you know that" Shy said while pulling out a syringe.

Shy went to the dresser and started putting together a farewell gift together for Tone. When he was done, he passed me the syringe.

"Give me your arm Tone," the tone in my voice let him know that his days were over.

Tone started crying harder while Shy wrapped a belt around his arm and searched for the biggest vein. I put the needle in his arm and pushed the heroin and rat poison into his body. At first, Tone smiled like he was in heaven. Then his body started convulsing and white foam started coming out his mouth. Me and Shy sat there and watched his fat ass die in pain.

"Let's get out of here God. We still got a couple mo' niggas to kill," Shy said.

He was right, as I turned around to leave

something caught my eye. "Hold up Shy," I said.

I went over to Fat Tone's body, and I pulled two keys off a chain around his neck. "What the fuck you think these is Shy?"

Shy walked up and grabbed the key out of my hand and examined it. "Oh, shit God, these two storage keys; It look like the storage place across 8 Mile on Greenfield".

He handed me the keys back, I placed them in my pocket, and we left. While Me and Shy left to go find Tommy and Gutta, I silently wondered what Tone fat ass had in the storage rooms. It had to be something important, or he wouldn't have had the keys on his neck. I would check, after I was done with Tommy and Gutta.

Tommy

Me and Gutta sat in a stolen G.M.C. truck watching a particular house for almost two hours. I received some solid information about the occupants of the house and since we couldn't come up with any other bright ideas, we decided unanimously that this was the only option. Neither one of us talked the whole time because there was nothing to talk about. Both my brothers and Bay Boy were dead, and somebody had to pay for it. I pulled out my throw away TracFone and I tried to call fat Tone, again. And once again, it went straight to voicemail. I promised myself right then and there that I was going to kill him, as soon as he came out of whatever hole he crawled in.

Gutta passed me a blunt of Purple Kush. I hit it as hard as I could and held it in until my lungs burned before I released it. I noticed an old Lincoln town car pulling up in front of the house and I got excited. "Aye, look there go the old bitch pullin up, Showtime."

I pulled my dreads back and put a skull cap over them. I made sure my 45 was locked and loaded as I exited the truck. I slowed down a bit to give the old lady enough time to get to the front door, then I went into action. I flew up the stairs and placed the gun to her back.

"I promise you if you scream or try something crazy imma kill yo old ass. You got that grandma?" She nodded her head.

"What do you want?" she asked.

"I want you to hurry up and open the fuckin door, it's cold as shit out here."

She did as she was told, and I entered the Livingroom to find it empty. I turned around just in time to see Gutta coming through the door with a Mac-90.

"Everything good cuz?" Gutta asked.

"Yea, I hear some music upstairs that's where that bitch at. Grab her and bring her down here," I said.

Gutta ran upstairs, while I removed the tape from my cargo pants and tied granny up. A few seconds later Gutta came down the stairs with a pretty ass red bone with boy shorts on. I looked down at her fat ass pussy and I felt my dick jump.

"Damn Trina, I didn't know you was layin like that. You look good enough to eat," I said smiling.

"Tommy what the fuck is you doin! Oh my God, you got my grandma tied up and everything what the fu…" **SLAAAP!**

"Shut the fuck up bitch. Bro, tie that bitch up and cover her mouth."

As Gutta tied her up, I walked through the Dining room and located the Kitchen. I opened the fridge up and after a couple of seconds I grabbed a Capri Sun and walked back to the Livingroom. Trina looked at me with fire in her eyes like she wanted to kill me.

"What, you wanted one to? Too bad this was the last one," I said. I grabbed a chair and sat down in front of Trina. "Look Trina, imma be short and sweet. This ain't got shit to do with you and everything to do with Ali. You can let some dick be the cause of me killin you and Ms. Orthopedic Shoes over here, or you can be smart and find a way for Ali to come here," I said.

Once she started crying hard as fuck, I knew I had her attention. "Where your phone at?" I asked.

She looked toward upstairs and Gutta quickly, ran up there to get it. I went back to the Kitchen to grab another Capri Sun. I noticed a bunch of Kitchen knives, so I grabbed one and went back to the Livingroom. Trina looked at me like I was crazy when I sat back down.

"Okay, I lied. But, this was the last one for real

this time," for some reason that made her Granny start crying extra hard.

Gutta came back downstairs with the phone, and he handed it to me. I snatched the tape off Trina's mouth hard as fuck.

"Tommy please don-"

"What's the password Trina?" I asked.

"3588"

I unlocked her phone went through the contacts, until I found Ali name. "Awww she got heart emoji by his name, ain't that cute?" I said mockingly.

I pushed his name and put the phone on speaker so I could hear the conversation. After about three rings he answered.

"What up babe?" Ali said.

"Nothing Love, I just miss you. I want to see you, where you at?

"I'm kind of busy right now. Can it wait till later?"

I pointed the gun at Trina and shook my head no.

"Ummm, no babe it can't. I'm hungry as shit and if I don't eat soon, I think imma die." Trina said.

The phone got quite for a minute then, Ali came back over the line.

"Fuuuck okay, give me an hour okay. I'll call you when I'm pulling up," Ali said.

"Okay, I love you."

"Love you, too." Then he hung up.

"I like the way you said, you was gone die

soon. Little do he know you're dead serious," I said laughing.

I covered her mouth back up and pulled out the Kitchen knife. Her eyes got big as fuck, I got up and cut her boy shorts right off her ass.

"Damn you thick as fuck! I always wanted to fuck you, anyway. Aye Gutta you got next?" I asked.

He smiled and nodded his head, like I knew he would. I flipped Trina on her stomach and pulled my dick out. Showtime!!!

INTIMIDATION

Chapter 13
Ali

As soon as I hung up the phone, I started punching the steering wheel. "Fuck! Fuck! Fuck! Fuck!" I screamed.

"What's the matter, God?" Shy asked me.

I had to take a couple of deep breaths before I could answer. "Somebody snatched Trina up Shy!"

"How the fuck you know? That was her who just called you?" Shy asked me.

"Yea Shy. And she used the code words I told her to use in case this ever happened," I said.

When I started fucking with Trina, everybody around me was dying because of the way I was living. So, I told her that if anybody snatched her and tried to get me to come to use the phrase "If I don't eat I'm going to die soon," and that would let me know that it was a set up.

"Damn God, it got to be Tommy."

"Yea, I figured that. That's why we've been sittin at their safe house for hours and ain't shit happened yet. Fuck!" I punched the steering wheel a couple of more times. It's starting to feel like everybody that's close to me gets hurt.

"So, what's the plan, God?" Shy asked me.

"I don't know Shy."

"You think she in on it?"

I didn't think of that. Now, I was though. I mean Brandy knew who Choppa was and they tried to set Shy up and I'm pretty sure, Trina knows Tommy because we're all from the same hood. How Tommy figure out that I was fucking with Trina is beyond me, but it didn't even matter now.

"I'm not really sure Shy but Fuck it! We been looking for them, now we know where they at. If anything, look fishy everybody can die," I said while starting up the car and pulling off.

We drove in silence all the way to Trina's house. Once I got close, I turned off my lights and stopped at the corner. "What you think?" I asked Shy.

"Our best play is to pull in through the alley and through the back of the house and pray like hell, ain't nobody watchin the backyard." Shy said. I was thinking the same thing.

I kept my lights out as we crept down the alley way pulling in behind Trina's house. I turned the car off and looked toward the back of the house.

"It look clear to me God," Shy said.

I watched the house for another two minutes before I felt satisfied. I popped the trunk, me and Shy both got out the car, and went to the back of the car.

"Look, Shy we don't know what we steppin into so let's be extra cautious. Put this vest on, grab that A.R., and grab a couple extra clips for yo 45,"

I said to shy. I put my vest on also and loaded up my weapons and bullets. I decided to use the choppa because that's what I was most familiar with. Me and Shy both walked through the fence that led us into the backyard and slowly, walked toward the backdoor. I tried to open it, but it was locked. I motioned for Shy to follow me so we could try the side door, but it was locked also. I was about to turn around when I heard something that caught my attention.

"You hear that Shy?"

"Yea, God. It sound like somebody fuckin," Shy said.

"Shy look at this shit," I said.

Shy looked through the window and shook his head. Tommy was fucking the shit out of Trina's grandmother, while Gutta sat at the window peeping through the blinds. Trina was on the floor naked, tied up, and crying. Without saying a word, I walked toward the front of the house, and I jumped over the side of the porch, so that Gutta couldn't see me. Shy climbed up behind me.

"Aye God, if you start shootin that yop threw the door, ain't no tell who you might hit."

I nodded my head in agreement. I pulled out my 40 and looked at Shy.

"Game time."

With that I quickly took two steps toward the window I Gutta standing at and opened fire. **BOC! BOC! BOC!** Shots fired and glass shattering, sent Shy into action. He kicked the front door open just in time to see Tommy turning the corner into the Dining room going toward the back door. I ran toward Trina and her Grandmother, while Shy took after Tommy.

"Shit, Shit, Fuck, I'm so sorry Trina don't say shit I got you." I said to Trina as I cut the tape off her wrist.

She spazzed out! "Fuck you Ali! Get the fuck off me I hate you," Trina said. She began helping her Grandmother up at the same time Shy walked back in.

"That pussy got away God. We missed him again," Shy said.

I heard coughing to my right, and I noticed Gutta was still alive. Shy raised the A.R. about to end his days, but I stopped him.

"Naw Shy! Not now, here go some tape tie his bitch ass up." I said.

Trina picked up her Grandmother and turned her attention toward me and Shy, "Get the fuck out my house now!!!"

"Come on Shy," I said. I can imagine why Trina so mad at me, but I warned her about my lifestyle, and she said, she didn't care. I guess when shit hit the fan the real came out of her.

Me and Shy both carried Gutta to the car we had waiting in the alley. I popped the trunk and pulled out a long rope. Then I looked at Gutta, "where Tommy goin?" that's all I cared about right now. Gutta snorted real hard then spit a big glob of blood on my shirt. Shy kicked him hard as shit in his face. "Oh, you a tough guy huh?" I asked getting more pissed by the minute. I tied the rope around his legs in a tight knot. "So, you still ain't talkin huh?" I asked.

"Suck my dick nigga!!! You can save that intimidation for somebody who scared of you pussy, do what you gone do." Gutta said.

"Damn Shy this nigga got heart, don't he? Cover his mouth with the tape," I said. Shy covered Gutta mouth with the tape, while I tied the other end of the rope to the trailer hitch on the car. "Yea, I know how to handle tough guys." I said.

I started the car up, put it in drive, and burnt rubber out the alley. I drove in circles around the hood for 20 minutes straight. When we got bored we parked the car and wiped it down. Then we went to find Tommy.

Tommy

I sat in a vacant house looking out the window with tears coming down my face. I wasn't crying because they got Gutta. I mean Gutta was like family to me and I'm hurt that he's dead; just like my brother and Bay Boy; but the real reason I'm crying is because I watched them kill Gutta and I couldn't do shit about it. I was so preoccupied with fucking Trina and her Grandma, that I let my guard down. Once the shots started and the door got kicked in, I didn't have enough time to grab my choppa off the floor. I ran to the back room and dove through the back window. I saw Shy come out and run in a totally different direction. I jumped the fence and hid in this vacant house. I watched them drag Gutta out to the alley. I watched them tie him up and in reality, I know that my brother's, Juice, Bay Boy, and Gutta looking up to me from Hell real disappointed, and I don't blame them.

I sat in the vacant house for a couple of hours until I felt like it was safe to leave. I walked a couple of blocks over, until I spotted an old Buick LA saber. I hotwired it, then drove all the way to the Safe House. Some people call it being paranoid, some people call it fear, I call it killers' instinct. You call it what you want, but something made me get out the car a couple blocks over. Our Safe House was in Hamtramck, to my knowledge no one knows about it, but better being safe than sorry. I crept through the backyard behind the Safe House and jumped the fence into our backyard. I found an open window in the back of the house and climbed through it. I kept silent for a minute, just listening, ...? sounds. After I was satisfied no one was here I walked over to the dresser to grab another shit bag. My shit bag bust when I went through the window, and I've been smelling like shit ever since. I kept the house dark as I made my way to the shower to wash up. The hot water relaxed me and helped me think clear. After I was done in the shower, I grabbed an all-black Jordan sweat suit. I navigated through the house in the dark all the way in the basement.

Once downstairs, I walked to the bar and

poured me a shot of Remy 1738. Then, I went behind the bar and picked up my brother Juice's A.R. 15 with the Mickey Mouse drums on it. I remember when he got it, I never seen him so happy. He never even shot it before. "Don't worry big bro, imma put this bitch to use for you," I said. And I meant that.

I walked back upstairs to the Livingroom and peeped out the blinds. I looked up and down the street and everything looked normal. I was about to walk away when something caught my eye. A black F-150 sat a couple houses down looked out of place. When you spend a lot of time at a house, you start to get familiar with the cars that line the block, and for some reason the F-150 sent me from 0 to 100 real quick. I ran toward the back room and opened the closest door to grab the vest.

I started turning on all the lights, as I walked to the back to snort coke. I made two big lines and snorted them hard as shit. The coke had me feeling invincible and I liked it. I thought I heard voices, so I ran back to the Livingroom. I didn't even have to look out the window to know the police was outside. I could clearly see the red and blue lights "Shiiiit!" I ran back to the bedroom and snorted two more lines, then I came back to the Livingroom and picked up the A.R.

I opened the door and I saw two police cars. Two of the cops were talking to the man across the street, when he pointed at me. I opened the front door wider and swung the A.R. back and forth. **BOC! BOC! BOC! BOC! BOC! BOC! BOC!** While they were too busy ducking behind cars, I used the distraction for me to jump off the porch and run toward the side of the house. As I ran down the side street anther cop car turned the corner. What you think I did? Better yet, let me show you. **BOC! BOC! BOC! BOC! BOC!** The police car fish talked into a pole. I cut threw a couple of houses and backyards, until I got a couple of blocks over. I heard a helicopter in the distance, so I decided to get rid of the A.R. in a garbage can. I took off the sweater I had on and the vest, then threw both of them in the trash can, also. I jumped another fence to the next block then began walking up the block. On cue a police officer came riding up the street, they slowed down, and placed the light on me.

"It's kind of chilly for you to be walking without a coat, ain't it son?" one of the officers asked.

"I enjoy the cold weather sir," I said in the calmest voice I could muster. Without warning the police swerved their car my way in order to block my path, then they both jumped out.

"Freeze, get the fuck on the ground."

"Okay damn don't shoot! I'll never leave my coat at home again," I said. The officer responded by kicking me in the face. Off to jail I go, I guess.

Mario

I sat in my plush condo in the suburban area of Westland, not that far from Detroit. I looked at the brown skin beauty on her knees sucking my dick and chest swelled with pride. I'm at the top of my heroin game and I have a bad bitch by my side. I'm not going to lie, I only really knew Jasmine for a couple of weeks, but the way she made me feel ain't no mistaking she's Wifey material. I felt my nuts swell and I knew I was about to come. I grabbed the back of Jasmine's head and made her deep throat my whole dick. When I finally did come, she didn't waste a drop.

"You like that baby? Jasmine asked me.

"Come on now, you know that." I responded coolly.

"Good got a surprise for you baby, I'll be right back."

"Don't take long," I told her.

"I won't."

I watched Jasmine's ass bounce, while she walked out and I felt my dick getting hard, again. I closed my eyes and laid back on the couch thinking about Fat Tone. I kicked myself for letting him swindle me out of 100 keys of heroin. With all the expenses I have because of the lifestyle I live; 100 keys is a debt I just couldn't pay back. While in deep thought, I felt a pair of strong arms grab me around my neck. My eyes popped open, and I realized, I was surrounded by a group of dangerous looking men. Jasmine stood in the middle of them. If looks could kill, she would've been dead by the daggers I shot her way. Just when I thought things couldn't get any worst, the Devil himself walked in the room. Mr.

David Corzilius AKA Don Corzilius. The guy who was choking me removed his arms.

"Bow to The Don," the guard said.

I got off the couch and got on my knees. The Don stuck his fist out and I kissed his ring. The big bodyguard grabbed me off the floor and placed me back on the couch.

"I've been hearing a lot of disappointing things about you Mario," Don Corzilius said.

"I don't understand Don Corzilius, what are these things that you heard?"

"Oh, I don't' know, just that you seem to have misplaced 100 kilos of mine."

I knew right then that Jasmine had to tell him that. It also dawned on me that it wasn't a coincidence that I met Jasmine, she was here to watch me. "I've got my best men on it, Don. I'll have the work back shortly," I said.

The Don tossed a newspaper at me. The first thing I saw was Fat Tone's face next to a woman's face, both were found dead in her apartment.

"You were saying?" The Don said.

I tried to respond, but the Don moved with lightning speed and slapped the shit out of me.

SLAAAP!

"Don't fucking say another word Mario! You have seven days, bring me my money or heroin and just to show you I'm not playing..."

The Don snapped his fingers, and another guard walked my best friend and bodyguard into the room. "I'm sorry boss." Those were the last words

Soto got to say before the guard blew half of his head off with a 357 revolver. His body hit the ground with a load thud.

"Have I made myself clear?"

"Yes, Don."

"Good! Jasmine will stay here to watch you." And with that, the Don and his goonies left the house.

Shy

I sat in a cheap motel called the Maury Hill on 8 Mile. I've been in here for 3 days straight drinking, smoking, and fucking. Ever since me and Ali tried to whack Tommy and it backfired twice in one night, I been chillin. Tommy almost got us together when he came out the Safe House shooting that chop. Luckily, I was driving, and I spotted him first or we would've died. After we found out Tommy was locked up me and Ali both decided to chill back, and peace out lives back together. Ali's my man, but no matter how tough he tries to act, I know that he's hurting inside. I mean, his whole family is dead and now his girl don't even want to talk to him. Me on the other hand, I never had a family anyway and besides losing Mark it's still a regular day for me. I heard a knock on the door, so I grabbed my gun and went to it.

"Who is it?" I yelled.

"It's me baby."

I opened the door and let a sexy ass diva

ANDRE CALVIN LEE JR

through the door.

"What took you so long Jasmine?"

"You know how hard it is to find a liquor store over here, damn. But, I got yo Remy," Jasmine said.

I met Jasmine 3 days ago and since I didn't trust her enough to take her to my spot this where we been. I ain't gone lie she cool as fuck, but after the situation with Brandy I got to say on point. "Lay down baby, let me suck your dick." Jasmine said all sexy like, so I did just that. Jasmine's head game was on a thousand. While Jasmine was sucking my dick, something clicked in my mind that made me open my eyes and clutch my gun. Before Jasmine went to the store, I gave her the door key...

Right on time, the motel door opened, I jumped up, grabbed Jasmine, and put the 45 to her head. "Come closer, imma open this hoe up." I said as I watch the room fill up with well-armed gwalla gwalla looking muthafuckas.

"Be my guest, she set me up first."

"Fuck you, Mario." Jasmine spit.

"No thank you tuts," Mario said back.

"Man fuck all that shit, God. Who the fuck is you and what you want?" I asked getting tired of the bullshit.

"My name is Mario, I used to distribute work to Big Rome and Fat Tone." Mario said in an irritated like manner.

"And what the fuck that got to do with me?" I asked getting heated.

"Recently, Fat Tone took 100 kilos of heroin

from me. I have solid information that says you and Ali killed him. All I want is my money or drugs your choice," Mario said.

"I don't know what the fuck you talkin about God. Yea we killed him, but we ain't get no work from him especially no 100 keys," I said. Almost as an after-thought I remembered the key of heroin that was on the dresser when we killed him.

A cellphone started ringing and Mario tossed it to me. "It's for you."

Curiosity got the best of me, so I picked it up making sure I kept Jasmine in my grip. "Hello"

"Ali is that you?"

Fuck! I realized the voice instantly. "Naw Trina this Shy, you okay?" I asked.

"No, Shy. These people got me, and my grandma and I'm scared. Where is Ali?

"I'm not sure Trina, but you know imma find him."

"Please hurry up Shy, I'm pregnant. I was gone tell him right before they snatched me up." Trina yelled through tears. The phone hung up and one of Mario's goons tossed a picture on the bed. I looked down at it was an ultrasound.

"Tell Ali he has 48 hours to get me my drugs or money, or I kill all three of them. The grandma, the girl, and the unborn child," with that being said, everybody started backing out of the small motel room. "If you don't mind, let the girl go please," Mario said.

I looked him dead in the eyes. "No deal. This

hoe good as dead," I said.

Mario stared at me for a second then smiled, "Like I said, be my guest."

"Fuck you Mario, I hope the Don kills yo ass!" Jasmine screamed.

I tossed her ass on the bed, then opened up her head, as I promised.

BOC!

I found my phone and called Ali. "What up Shy? I thought you was chillin, what's wrong Shy?" Ali asked me.

"Call Cook, we gone need all the guns we can get."

To be continued....

ABOUT THE AUTHOR

Andre Calvin Lee Jr

Andre Calvin Lee Jr also known as "Lil Dre, Drizz, or CJ" is a talented literary, a light shining Libra and testament, born and raised in Detroit Michigan carrying a loving heart for loyalty. Naturally gifted at writing, he developed a rap persona and wrote music. Through his life living in his neighborhood, he grew an education through school and detention centers. He utilized being selfishly self-made to navigate a life to have what he wanted and not care about living but, you cannot stop destiny. Through dedication, a support system, and a sound mind he has created a legacy with his knowledge. Knowing being naturally gifted is not enough, he developed his first book "Who Let the Animal Out?". Knowing now that being in a damaging cycle is a choice of insanity, this "started from the bottom" soul, will prosper and keep producing material and leveling up so, watch out for what's coming next!

Made in the USA
Columbia, SC
24 March 2024

33237290R00078